The Alchemist's Legacy

Elena Rayne

Contents

Chapter 1

Liora stood at the edge of her father's study, the familiar scent of old books and parchment wafting around her. The room was filled with memories, each corner holding a fragment of her childhood. She had spent countless hours here, watching her father work on his mysterious projects, never quite understanding the full extent of his studies. Now, with his sudden passing, the room felt both comforting and daunting.

Her father's funeral had been a small, somber affair. The townspeople of Elaria had come to pay their respects, offering condolences and sharing stories of the man they had known. Liora had listened politely, her mind preoccupied with the weight of her new responsibilities. As the sole heir, she had inherited the family estate, a sprawling manor on the outskirts of the town. But along with the physical property, she had also inherited something far more enigmatic—her father's secrets.

After the last of the mourners had left, Liora found herself drawn back to the study. She had avoided this room since his death, unable to face the flood of emotions it brought. But now, standing in the doorway, she knew she couldn't postpone it any longer. Her father had always been a private man, and she suspected that the answers to many of her questions lay hidden within these walls.

Taking a deep breath, she stepped inside and closed the door behind her. The room was just as he had left it, cluttered with books, scrolls, and various instruments she couldn't name. The large oak desk was piled high with papers, and a worn leather chair stood behind it, its cushions bearing the imprint of countless hours of use. Liora approached the desk, her fingers trailing over the surface as she took in the scene.

She had always known her father was an alchemist, though he had never shared much about his work. Alchemy had been a respected and revered art in Elaria once, but over the years, it had faded into obscurity. Many considered it little more than a myth, a relic of a bygone era. Her father, however, had remained dedicated to his craft, often disappearing for days at a time into his study or the basement laboratory she was forbidden to enter.

Liora sat down in the chair, feeling its familiar comfort. She glanced at the papers on the desk, her eyes catching on a particular scroll. It was sealed with a wax emblem she didn't recognize, and curiosity got the better of her. She broke the seal and unrolled the parchment, revealing intricate diagrams and notes written in her father's meticulous hand.

As she read, a mixture of confusion and fascination filled her. The notes detailed complex formulas and experiments, references to elements and compounds she had never heard of. Her father had been working on something significant, something far beyond her understanding. The more she read, the more she realized that alchemy was not just an ancient myth—it was real, and her father had been a master of the craft.

Among the papers, she found a letter addressed to her. Her heart pounded as she unfolded it, recognizing her father's handwriting.

"My dearest Liora," it began. "If you are reading this, it means I am no longer with you. There are things I have kept from you, not out of mistrust, but to protect you. Our family has a legacy, one that is both powerful and dangerous. You are now the keeper of this legacy, and it is imperative that you understand its importance."

Liora's hands trembled as she continued reading. The letter explained that her father had been working on an alchemical formula capable of immense power, a formula that could either save or destroy. He had hidden his work to keep it from falling into the wrong hands, knowing that many would seek to use it for their own gain.

"You have the potential to continue my work," the letter concluded. "But you must be careful. Trust no one, and seek out those who can guide you. The future of Elaria may depend on your success."

Tears blurred her vision as she finished the letter. The weight of her father's words settled heavily on her shoulders. She had always felt there was something more to him, a depth she couldn't quite reach. Now, she understood the magnitude of his burden and the responsibility he had passed on to her.

Determined to honor her father's legacy, Liora spent the next few days immersing herself in his notes and experiments. She quickly realized she was out of her depth. The alchemical texts were complex, filled with references to ancient knowledge and practices that had been forgotten by most. She needed help, and she needed it soon.

One evening, as she was poring over a particularly challenging formula, there was a knock at the door. Liora hesitated, her father's warning echoing in her mind. Trust no one. But she couldn't do this alone. Gathering her courage, she went to the door and opened it.

A tall, hooded figure stood on the threshold, illuminated by the soft glow of the setting sun. The stranger removed his hood, revealing a man with striking green eyes and an air of quiet confidence.

"Liora," he said, his voice gentle but firm. "My name is Kael. I was a friend of your father's. I believe I can help you."

Liora studied him for a moment, searching for any sign of deceit. But there was something in his eyes, a sincerity that she couldn't ignore. She stepped aside, allowing him to enter.

Kael walked into the study, his gaze sweeping over the room before settling on her. "Your father was a great man," he said softly. "And a brilliant alchemist. He believed you have the potential to carry on his work."

Liora nodded, still wary but willing to listen. "He left me his notes, but I don't understand most of it. I need guidance."

Kael smiled, a hint of sadness in his eyes. "That's why I'm here. Your father entrusted me with his secrets, and I will do my best to help you. But you must be prepared for the challenges ahead. Alchemy is not just about knowledge—it's about strength, courage, and the willingness to face the unknown."

Liora took a deep breath, feeling a renewed sense of determination. "I'm ready," she said. "Tell me where to begin."

With Kael's guidance, Liora embarked on her journey into the world of alchemy. The road ahead was uncertain and filled with dangers, but she knew she was not alone. Together, they would uncover the mysteries of her father's work and face whatever challenges came their way.

And so, the legacy of the alchemist began anew, with a young woman determined to honor her father's memory and protect her world from the looming threat.

Chapter 2

Liora awoke to the soft light of dawn filtering through her window, casting a warm glow over her room. She stretched and rubbed her eyes, the events of the previous day flooding back to her. Kael's arrival had brought a mixture of relief and apprehension. His promise to help her navigate the complexities of alchemy was reassuring, but she knew the journey ahead would be anything but easy.

After a quick breakfast, Liora made her way to her father's study. Kael was already there, examining one of the alchemical texts spread out on the desk. He looked up as she entered, offering her a small, encouraging smile.

"Good morning, Liora," he said. "I've been going through some of your father's notes. There's a lot to unpack here, but we'll take it one step at a time."

Liora nodded, feeling a mixture of excitement and nervousness. "Where do we start?"

Kael gestured to the array of books and scrolls. "Your father was meticulous in his record-keeping. We'll begin with the basics, ensuring you have a solid understanding of fundamental alchemical principles before we move on to more advanced concepts. Alchemy is as much about philosophy and understanding the natural world as it is about mixing potions and casting spells."

He picked up a thick tome bound in worn leather and handed it to her. "This is 'The Foundations of Alchemy,' one of the core texts your father relied on. It covers the basic theories and practices you'll need to master."

Liora took the book, feeling its weight in her hands. She opened it to the first page, her eyes scanning the elegant script. The introduction spoke of alchemy as the pursuit of transformation and enlightenment, a blending of science, magic, and art. It was a discipline that required patience, dedication, and a deep respect for the natural order.

As she delved into the text, Kael began explaining key concepts. "Alchemy is built on the principle of transmutation," he said. "The idea that all matter can be transformed from one state to another. It's not just about turning lead into gold—that's a common misconception. True alchemy involves understanding the fundamental properties of materials and harnessing their potential for transformation."

Liora listened intently, her mind racing to absorb the information. She read about the Four Elements—Earth, Water, Fire, and Air—and their role in alchemical processes. Each element had unique properties and correspondences, and mastering their manipulation was crucial to any alchemist's success.

Kael demonstrated a simple exercise, combining water and a few drops of an herbal extract to create a glowing, luminescent liquid. "This is a basic elixir of light," he explained. "It's one of the first concoctions every alchemist learns. It teaches control and precision, as even a slight miscalculation can cause the mixture to fail."

Liora watched in awe as the liquid shimmered in the vial, casting a soft, ethereal glow. She couldn't wait to try it herself, feeling a surge of determination to prove herself worthy of her father's legacy.

Over the next few days, Liora and Kael settled into a routine. They spent their mornings studying the alchemical texts, discussing theories and principles. Afternoons were dedicated to practical exercises, with Kael guiding Liora through the creation of simple potions and elixirs. Despite the challenges, Liora found herself growing more confident with each passing day.

One afternoon, while working on an elixir of healing, Liora stumbled upon a hidden compartment in her father's desk. Intrigued, she carefully pried it open to reveal a collection of handwritten journals. The leather-bound volumes were filled with her father's personal notes and observations, offering a glimpse into his private thoughts and experiments.

Kael joined her as she began reading through the journals. "These are invaluable," he said. "Your father's insights and experiences will be crucial in understanding the more advanced aspects of alchemy."

The journals revealed a man driven by a relentless pursuit of knowledge, dedicated to uncovering the mysteries of the universe. Her father had experimented with a wide range of alchemical processes, from creating powerful elixirs to transmuting base metals into precious ones. He had documented his successes and failures with meticulous detail, providing a roadmap for Liora to follow.

One entry caught her attention. It spoke of an ancient alchemical formula, a legendary elixir known as the "Essence of Eternity." According to her father's notes, this elixir had the potential to grant immense power and immortality. However, it was incredibly dangerous, and its creation required rare and potent ingredients.

Liora's heart raced as she read the entry. The Essence of Eternity sounded like something out of a fairy tale, but her father had believed in its existence. He had spent years searching for the ingredients and perfecting the formula, but his notes indicated that he had never completed it.

"This is incredible," Liora said, her voice filled with awe. "My father was working on something truly extraordinary. The Essence of Eternity... it sounds impossible."

Kael nodded, his expression serious. "It is a formidable goal, one that many alchemists have sought throughout history. But it's also incredibly dangerous. The power it grants can corrupt even the purest of hearts. Your father understood the risks, and that's why he kept his work hidden."

Liora closed the journal, her mind racing with possibilities. The discovery of her father's secret research added a new layer of complexity to her journey. She knew she couldn't pursue the Essence of Eternity without fully understanding its implications and mastering the fundamental principles of alchemy.

As the days turned into weeks, Liora continued her studies with renewed vigor. Kael proved to be an excellent teacher, patient and knowledgeable. Under his guidance, she learned to transmute simple metals, create potent elixirs, and harness the elemental forces of nature.

One evening, as they were working on a particularly challenging experiment, Kael shared a bit of his own story. He had been an apprentice to a master alchemist in a distant land, dedicating his life to the pursuit of alchemical knowledge. When he heard of Liora's father and his remarkable discoveries, he had journeyed to Elaria to learn from him. Though their time together had been brief, Kael had gained invaluable insights and a deep respect for the man.

"Your father was a genius," Kael said, his voice filled with admiration. "He had a way of seeing the world that was truly unique. His understanding of alchemy went beyond formulas and potions. He believed in the potential for transformation and enlightenment, not just of materials, but of the human spirit."

Liora felt a pang of loss, missing her father more than ever. But she also felt a deep sense of pride. She was determined to honor his memory and continue his work, no matter the challenges.

One night, as she was preparing for bed, Liora couldn't shake the feeling that she was being watched. She glanced around the room, her eyes scanning the shadows. Everything seemed normal, but her instincts told her otherwise. She dismissed the feeling as paranoia, a side effect of the intense study and the weight of her new responsibilities.

However, the sense of unease persisted over the following days. Strange things began to happen—books would move from their places, ingredients would go missing, and Liora would catch glimpses of shadowy figures out of the corner of her eye. She shared her concerns with Kael, who took them seriously.

"We must be cautious," he said. "There are those who would go to great lengths to possess your father's knowledge. We cannot afford to let our guard down."

Determined to protect her father's legacy, Liora and Kael took measures to secure the manor. They set up wards and protective charms around the property, and Kael began training Liora in defensive alchemical techniques. The threat of danger only strengthened her resolve, and she threw herself into her studies with renewed determination.

As Liora continued to unravel the secrets of alchemy, she discovered a profound connection to the craft. The more she learned, the more she felt in tune with the natural world and its elemental forces. Alchemy was not just about manipulation—it was about harmony, balance, and understanding the intricate web of life.

One afternoon, while working on a particularly delicate transmutation, Liora felt a sudden surge of energy. Her hands moved with precision and confidence, the process flowing seamlessly. When the experiment was complete, she stared in amazement at the flawless result.

Kael, who had been observing, nodded in approval. "You're becoming a true alchemist, Liora. Your father would be proud."

Liora smiled, feeling a sense of accomplishment. She knew there was still much to learn and many challenges ahead, but she was ready to face them. With Kael by her side and her father's legacy as her guide, she was determined to master the art of alchemy and protect the kingdom of Elaria.

The secrets of alchemy were no longer a mystery—they were her destiny.

Chapter 3

Liora woke with the dawn, her mind buzzing with the revelations and lessons from the previous days. The journey into the world of alchemy was proving to be more profound and complex than she had ever imagined. Each day brought new challenges and discoveries, and she felt both exhilarated and overwhelmed by the weight of her new responsibilities.

Kael was already in the study when she arrived, arranging various ingredients and tools on the large oak desk. His presence had become a comforting constant in her life, and his guidance invaluable. He looked up as she entered, his green eyes warm with encouragement.

"Good morning, Liora," he said, smiling. "Today, we'll begin your first practical lessons in alchemy. You've learned the theories and principles; now it's time to apply them."

Liora nodded, feeling a mix of excitement and nervousness. She approached the desk, where Kael had laid out an array of vials, herbs, and minerals. The tools of an alchemist, she thought, marveling at the possibilities they represented.

Kael handed her a small mortar and pestle. "We'll start with something simple—a basic healing salve. It's an essential skill for any alchemist and a good exercise in combining ingredients."

He guided her through the process, explaining the properties of each ingredient and how they interacted with one another. Liora crushed dried herbs, mixed them with powdered minerals, and carefully added drops of essential oils. Under Kael's watchful eye, she followed the steps meticulously, her hands steady and precise.

As she worked, Kael shared more about the philosophy of alchemy. "Alchemy is about transformation," he said. "Not just of materials, but of oneself. It requires patience, intuition, and a deep understanding of the natural world. Every ingredient, every element, has its own unique properties and potential. The alchemist's role is to unlock that potential."

Liora listened intently, absorbing his words. She could feel the truth in them, a resonance that went beyond intellectual understanding. Alchemy was indeed a path of transformation, a journey that mirrored her own growth and self-discovery.

When the salve was complete, Kael inspected it carefully. He nodded in approval, his expression one of quiet pride. "Well done, Liora. This is an excellent first effort. You have a natural talent for alchemy."

Liora felt a surge of satisfaction and relief. The process had been challenging, but also deeply rewarding. She was beginning to understand why her father had been so dedicated to his craft, and why he had kept it hidden. Alchemy was a powerful and profound art, one that required both skill and wisdom.

Over the next few days, Liora continued her practical training, experimenting with various potions and elixirs. She learned to create tinctures for healing, tonics for strength, and even simple charms for protection. Each success boosted her confidence, while each failure taught her valuable lessons in patience and perseverance.

One afternoon, Kael decided it was time to introduce her to elemental transmutation, a cornerstone of alchemical practice. They moved to the basement laboratory, a space that had always been off-limits to her. As she descended the stone steps, Liora felt a thrill of anticipation. This was where her father had conducted his most important experiments, where the true heart of his work lay.

The laboratory was a cavernous room, filled with shelves of ancient books, jars of mysterious substances, and intricate apparatuses. In the center stood a large workbench, covered with alchemical symbols and markings. Kael led her to the bench, his demeanor serious and focused.

"Elemental transmutation involves changing the properties of one element into another," he explained. "It's a delicate and complex process, requiring precise control and a deep understanding of elemental properties. Today, we'll start with a basic exercise—transmuting copper into silver."

He placed a small piece of copper on the workbench, then handed Liora a set of alchemical tools. "Follow my instructions carefully. This process requires concentration and precision."

Liora took a deep breath and nodded, her hands steady as she began the process. She mixed various substances, following Kael's guidance, and applied them to the copper. As she worked, she could feel the energy of the elements responding to her touch, a subtle but powerful force that flowed through her.

The final step involved a complex series of gestures and incantations, channeling the elemental energy into the copper. Liora focused intently, her mind and body aligned with the process. As she completed the final gesture, a soft glow enveloped the copper, and it began to change.

She watched in awe as the dull, reddish metal transformed into bright, gleaming silver. The transmutation was complete. She had successfully changed one element into another, a feat that felt both miraculous and deeply satisfying.

Kael smiled, his eyes filled with pride. "You did it, Liora. This is a significant achievement. Elemental transmutation is one of the most challenging aspects of alchemy, and you've mastered it on your first attempt."

Liora felt a profound sense of accomplishment. The journey had only just begun, but she was already making strides. She understood now why her father had dedicated his life to alchemy. It was a path of endless discovery, a journey of transformation and enlightenment.

That evening, as they sat by the fireplace, Kael shared stories of his own training and experiences. He spoke of ancient alchemical orders, hidden knowledge, and the quest for the philosopher's stone, a legendary artifact said to grant unlimited power and wisdom.

"Your father was searching for the philosopher's stone," Kael said, his voice thoughtful. "He believed it held the key to unlocking the full potential of alchemy. His research brought him closer than anyone in centuries, but he also understood the dangers. That's why he kept his work hidden."

Liora listened, her mind filled with questions. The philosopher's stone sounded like a myth, but she knew better than to dismiss it outright. Her father's notes had already revealed truths she had once thought impossible.

"What do you think, Kael?" she asked. "Is the philosopher's stone real? Can it be found?"

Kael considered her question for a moment. "I believe it's real," he said finally. "But finding it requires more than just knowledge and skill. It requires a pure heart and a noble purpose. The stone is said to grant its power only to those who are truly worthy."

Liora nodded, pondering his words. The quest for the philosopher's stone was a daunting prospect, but it also felt like a natural extension of her journey. She was determined to honor her father's legacy, and if the stone held the key to understanding the full potential of alchemy, she would seek it out.

As the weeks passed, Liora's skills continued to grow. She mastered more complex potions, refined her transmutation techniques, and delved deeper into the ancient texts. Her bond with Kael also deepened, their shared dedication to alchemy creating a strong and unbreakable connection.

One day, while working on a particularly challenging elixir, Liora experienced a breakthrough. She had been struggling with the formula for days, unable to get the proportions right. Frustrated, she took a break and went for a walk in the nearby forest.

As she wandered among the trees, she felt a sudden inspiration. The forest was alive with elemental energy, a perfect balance of earth, water, fire, and air. She realized that the key to the elixir lay in understanding this balance, in harmonizing the elements rather than forcing them together.

Returning to the laboratory, Liora applied her newfound insight. She adjusted the formula, focusing on creating harmony rather than control. As she completed the final step, the elixir glowed with a brilliant light, its energy pure and powerful.

Kael, who had been observing, nodded in approval. "You've done it, Liora. You've grasped the true essence of alchemy. It's not about dominance—it's about balance and harmony."

Liora felt a deep sense of fulfillment. She was beginning to understand the deeper truths of alchemy, the wisdom that her father had sought to impart. Her journey was far from over, but she was on the right path.

That night, as she lay in bed, Liora thought about the road ahead. There were still many challenges to face, many mysteries to unravel. But she felt ready, confident in her abilities and supported by Kael's guidance.

Her father's legacy was a heavy burden, but it was also a gift. Through alchemy, she was discovering her true self, transforming not just materials, but her own spirit. The path of the alchemist was one of endless discovery, and she was determined to walk it with courage and wisdom.

As she drifted off to sleep, Liora knew that the journey had only just begun. But with each step, she was becoming stronger, wiser, and more attuned to the magical world of alchemy. And with Kael by her side, she felt ready to face whatever challenges lay ahead.

Chapter 4

The days passed swiftly as Liora immersed herself in the study of alchemy. Her skills grew with each lesson, her confidence bolstered by Kael's patient guidance. Yet, even as she delved deeper into her father's work, the sense of unease persisted. She couldn't shake the feeling that she was being watched, that unseen eyes were tracking her every move.

One evening, as the sun dipped below the horizon, casting long shadows across the manor, Liora decided to take a break from her studies. She needed fresh air and a moment to clear her mind. Pulling a shawl around her shoulders, she stepped outside into the cool twilight.

The gardens surrounding the manor were a serene haven, filled with fragrant blooms and the soft rustle of leaves. Liora wandered along the stone paths, her thoughts drifting back to her father and the mysteries he had left behind. She felt a pang of longing, wishing he were here to guide her.

Lost in her reverie, she didn't notice the figure approaching until it was almost upon her. Startled, she turned to find a tall man standing at the edge of the garden, partially obscured by the shadows. He wore a long cloak, the hood pulled low over his face.

"Who are you?" Liora demanded, her voice tinged with both curiosity and caution.

The stranger stepped forward, removing his hood to reveal striking green eyes that seemed to glimmer in the fading light. His features were sharp and well-defined, his expression serious but not unkind.

"My name is Kael," he said, his voice deep and resonant. "I was a friend of your father's. I've come to offer my help."

Liora's heart skipped a beat. This was the mysterious stranger her father had mentioned in his letter. She had been expecting him, but now that he was here, she felt a mixture of relief and apprehension.

"How do I know I can trust you?" she asked, her eyes narrowing slightly.

Kael smiled faintly, a gesture that softened his stern demeanor. "Your father and I worked together on many alchemical projects. He trusted me with his secrets and his legacy. I understand your hesitation, but I assure you, I am here to help."

Liora studied him for a moment, searching his eyes for any sign of deceit. She saw only sincerity and a deep well of knowledge. Taking a deep breath, she nodded. "Alright, come inside. We have much to discuss."

Back in the study, Kael explained his connection to her father. He had been an apprentice to a master alchemist in a distant land, dedicating his life to the pursuit of alchemical knowledge. When he heard of Liora's father and his remarkable discoveries, he had journeyed to Elaria to learn from him. Though their time together had been brief, Kael had gained invaluable insights and a deep respect for the man.

"Your father was a genius," Kael said, his voice filled with admiration. "He had a way of seeing the world that was truly unique. His understanding of alchemy went beyond formulas and potions. He believed in the potential for transformation and enlightenment, not just of materials, but of the human spirit."

Liora listened, her mind filled with questions. "What brought you here now? Why did you wait until after his death to come forward?"

Kael's expression grew somber. "I was away on a quest, searching for rare ingredients for one of your father's experiments. By the time I returned, he had passed. I came as soon as I heard the news. I wanted to ensure his legacy was protected and to offer my assistance to you."

Liora felt a pang of sadness and gratitude. Her father's death had left a void in her life, but Kael's presence brought a sense of continuity and purpose. She knew she would need his guidance to navigate the complexities of alchemy and to uncover the secrets her father had left behind.

Over the next few days, Kael and Liora settled into a routine. They spent their mornings studying the alchemical texts, discussing theories and principles. Afternoons were dedicated to practical exercises, with Kael guiding Liora through the creation of more advanced potions and elixirs. Despite the challenges, Liora found herself growing more confident with each passing day.

One afternoon, while they were working on a particularly complex transmutation, Liora decided to broach a subject that had been on her mind. "Kael, have you ever heard of the Essence of Eternity?"

Kael's eyes widened slightly, a flicker of surprise crossing his face. "Yes, I have. It's a legendary elixir, said to grant immense power and immortality. Many alchemists have sought it, but few have come close to discovering its true nature."

Liora nodded, feeling a thrill of excitement. "My father was working on it. I found his notes, but the formula is incomplete. Do you think it's possible to finish it?"

Kael's expression grew thoughtful. "The Essence of Eternity is incredibly dangerous. Its power can corrupt even the purest of hearts. Your father understood the risks, which is why he kept his work hidden. If we are to pursue this, we must proceed with the utmost caution."

Liora felt a surge of determination. The Essence of Eternity was a daunting prospect, but it also felt like a natural extension of her journey. She was determined to honor her father's legacy, and if the elixir held the key to understanding the full potential of alchemy, she would seek it out.

As they continued their work, Liora and Kael formed a strong bond. Their shared dedication to alchemy created a deep connection, and Liora found herself increasingly relying on Kael's wisdom and support. He was not just a mentor, but a friend and confidant.

One evening, as they sat by the fireplace, Kael shared more about his past. He spoke of his training under a master alchemist, his travels in search of rare ingredients, and the many challenges he had faced. Liora listened, fascinated by his stories and the depth of his experience.

"Alchemy is a lifelong journey," Kael said, his voice thoughtful. "It's about more than just mixing potions and transmuting metals. It's about understanding the fundamental principles of the universe and seeking to harmonize with them. Your father believed in this, and so do I."

Liora felt a deep sense of connection to Kael's words. She was beginning to understand the true essence of alchemy, the wisdom that her father had sought to impart. Her journey was far from over, but she was on the right path.

That night, as she lay in bed, Liora thought about the road ahead. There were still many challenges to face, many mysteries to unravel. But she felt ready, confident in her abilities and supported by Kael's guidance.

Her father's legacy was a heavy burden, but it was also a gift. Through alchemy, she was discovering her true self, transforming not just materials, but her own spirit. The path of the alchemist was one of endless discovery, and she was determined to walk it with courage and wisdom.

As she drifted off to sleep, Liora knew that the journey had only just begun. But with each step, she was becoming stronger, wiser, and more attuned to the magical world of alchemy. And with Kael by her side, she felt ready to face whatever challenges lay ahead.

Chapter 5

Liora's days fell into a steady rhythm of study and practice, her mind and spirit becoming more attuned to the intricate dance of alchemy. Kael's presence provided a steadying influence, his wisdom and patience guiding her through the labyrinth of her father's work. Each lesson brought new challenges, pushing her to the limits of her abilities and beyond.

One morning, Kael introduced a new topic: elemental infusion. It was a complex process, involving the manipulation of elemental energies to enhance the properties of various substances. As he explained the principles, Liora listened intently, eager to learn.

"Elemental infusion requires a deep understanding of the elements and their interactions," Kael said, his voice calm and measured. "It's not just about mixing ingredients; it's about channeling the raw power of nature and harmonizing it with your intent."

He demonstrated by infusing a simple piece of iron with the essence of fire, transforming it into a glowing, radiant metal. The process was delicate and precise, requiring a steady hand and a focused mind. Liora watched in awe, her respect for Kael's skills growing with each demonstration.

When it was her turn, Liora approached the task with a mixture of excitement and trepidation. She chose to work with water, hoping to create a healing elixir that could soothe wounds and restore vitality. Following Kael's guidance, she carefully prepared the ingredients and began the infusion.

As she worked, she felt the elemental energy flow through her, a powerful current that seemed to resonate with her very being. The process was challenging, requiring intense concentration and control. But Liora persevered, her determination unwavering.

After several hours of meticulous effort, she completed the infusion. The result was a shimmering blue liquid that glowed with an inner light. Kael examined it, nodding in approval.

"You've done well, Liora," he said, his voice filled with pride. "This elixir has the potential to heal even the most grievous injuries. Your control over the elemental energies is impressive."

Liora felt a surge of satisfaction. The journey had been difficult, but the rewards were worth it. She was beginning to understand the true depth and power of alchemy, and she was eager to continue her studies.

As the days passed, Liora faced increasingly complex challenges. Kael introduced new concepts and techniques, each one more demanding than the last. She learned to transmute base metals into precious ones, to create protective charms, and to harness the power of the elements in ways she had never imagined.

One afternoon, while working on a particularly difficult transmutation, Liora encountered a setback. No matter how carefully she followed the instructions, the process seemed to fail at the final step. Frustrated, she set aside the materials and took a deep breath, trying to calm her racing thoughts.

Kael approached her, his expression sympathetic. "Every alchemist faces challenges, Liora," he said gently. "Failure is a part of the learning process. It's how we grow and improve. Take a step back, reflect on what went wrong, and try again."

Liora nodded, grateful for his encouragement. She took a moment to review her notes, looking for any mistakes or oversights. As she did, she realized that she had miscalculated the proportions of the ingredients. Determined to succeed. she adjusted the formula and began the process anew.

This time, the transmutation was a success. The base metal transformed into a gleaming silver, the result of her perseverance and dedication. Liora felt a profound sense of accomplishment, her confidence bolstered by the experience.

Kael smiled, his eyes filled with pride. "Well done, Liora. You've shown great resilience and determination. These qualities are just as important as knowledge and skill in the practice of alchemy."

As Liora's abilities grew, so did her understanding of the deeper principles of alchemy. She learned that it was not just about manipulating substances, but about harmonizing with the natural world and understanding the interconnectedness of all things. Each element, each ingredient, held a unique energy and potential, and the alchemist's role was to unlock and harness that potential.

One evening, as they sat by the fireplace, Kael shared more about his own journey. He spoke of his early struggles, the countless hours of study and practice, and the mentors who had guided him along the way.

"Alchemy is a path of continuous learning and growth," he said, his voice thoughtful. "It's a journey that requires patience, humility, and a willingness to embrace both success and failure. Your father understood this, and so do I."

Liora felt a deep sense of connection to Kael's words. She was beginning to see alchemy not just as a science, but as a philosophy, a way of understanding and interacting with the world. Her father's legacy was a gift, one that she was determined to honor and uphold.

As the weeks turned into months, Liora continued to hone her skills. She faced numerous challenges and setbacks, but each one only strengthened her resolve. With Kael's guidance, she learned to create powerful elixirs, transmute base metals into precious ones, and harness the elemental forces of nature.

One day, while working on a particularly complex formula, Liora discovered a hidden compartment in her father's desk. Inside was a collection of ancient texts, written in a language she couldn't decipher. Intrigued, she showed them to Kael.

"These are old alchemical manuscripts," he said, examining the texts. "They contain knowledge and secrets that have been passed down through generations. Your father must have been studying them in his quest for the Essence of Eternity."

Liora felt a thrill of excitement. The manuscripts were a treasure trove of alchemical knowledge, a link to the ancient traditions and wisdom of her craft. She was determined to unlock their secrets, to continue her father's work and uncover the mysteries of the Essence of Eternity.

With Kael's help, Liora began the painstaking process of translating the manuscripts. It was a daunting task, requiring not only linguistic skills but also a deep understanding of alchemical principles. But Liora was undeterred. She spent long hours poring over the texts, her mind racing with possibilities and insights.

As she worked, she felt a growing sense of connection to the ancient alchemists who had come before her. Their knowledge and wisdom were a part of her legacy, a legacy that she was determined to honor and uphold.

One evening, as she was translating a particularly difficult passage, Liora felt a sudden surge of inspiration. The words seemed to come alive, revealing a hidden meaning and a deeper truth. She realized that the key to the Essence of Eternity lay not just in the ingredients and formulas, but in the alchemist's own spirit and intent.

"Kael," she said excitedly, "I think I've found something. The Essence of Eternity isn't just a potion—it's a state of being, a harmony between the alchemist and the elements. It's about understanding and embracing the fundamental principles of transformation and enlightenment."

Kael's eyes widened with interest. "That's a profound insight, Liora. Your father was searching for more than just a powerful elixir. He was seeking a deeper understanding of the nature of existence and the true potential of alchemy."

Liora felt a deep sense of fulfillment. She was beginning to understand her father's vision, the wisdom that he had sought to impart. Her journey was far from over, but she was on the right path. With Kael's guidance and the knowledge of the ancient alchemists, she was determined to unlock the secrets of the Essence of Eternity and fulfill her father's legacy.

As the weeks turned into months, Liora's skills continued to grow. She faced numerous challenges and setbacks, but each one only strengthened her resolve. With Kael's guidance, she learned to create powerful elixirs, transmute base metals into precious ones, and harness the elemental forces of nature.

One day, while working on a particularly complex formula, Liora discovered a hidden compartment in her father's desk. Inside was a collection of ancient texts, written in a language she couldn't decipher. Intrigued, she showed them to Kael.

"These are old alchemical manuscripts," he said, examining the texts. "They contain knowledge and secrets that have been passed down through generations. Your father must have been studying them in his quest for the Essence of Eternity."

Liora felt a thrill of excitement. The manuscripts were a treasure trove of alchemical knowledge, a link to the ancient traditions and wisdom of her craft. She was determined to unlock their secrets, to continue her father's work and uncover the mysteries of the Essence of Eternity.

With Kael's help, Liora began the painstaking process of translating the manuscripts. It was a daunting task, requiring not only linguistic skills but also a deep understanding of alchemical principles. But Liora was undeterred. She spent long hours poring over the texts, her mind racing with possibilities and insights.

As she worked, she felt a growing sense of connection to the ancient alchemists who had come before her. Their knowledge and wisdom were a part of her legacy, a legacy that she was determined to honor and uphold.

One evening, as she was translating a particularly difficult passage, Liora felt a sudden surge of inspiration. The words seemed to come alive, revealing a hidden meaning and a deeper truth. She realized that the key to the Essence of Eternity lay not just in the ingredients and formulas, but in the alchemist's own spirit and intent.

"Kael," she said excitedly, "I think I've found something. The Essence of Eternity isn't just a potion—it's a state of being, a harmony between the alchemist and the elements. It's about understanding and embracing the fundamental principles of transformation and enlightenment."

Kael's eyes widened with interest. "That's a profound insight, Liora. Your father was searching for more than just a powerful elixir. He was seeking a deeper understanding of the nature of existence and the true potential of alchemy."

Liora felt a deep sense of fulfillment. She was beginning to understand her father's vision, the wisdom that he had sought to impart. Her journey was far from over, but she was on the right path. With Kael's guidance and the knowledge of the ancient alchemists, she was determined to unlock the secrets of the Essence of Eternity and fulfill her father's legacy.

As the days turned into weeks, Liora's confidence grew. She faced each new challenge with determination and resilience, knowing that she was on the path to mastering the true essence of alchemy. With Kael's unwavering support and the legacy of her father guiding her, she felt ready to face whatever lay ahead.

The lessons were demanding, but they also brought a deep sense of fulfillment. Liora knew that she was not just learning a craft; she was transforming herself, becoming the alchemist her father had always believed she could be. And as she stood at the threshold of new discoveries, she felt a profound sense of purpose and destiny.

Her journey had only just begun, but Liora knew that she was ready. With Kael by her side and the wisdom of the ancients to guide her, she would unlock the secrets of alchemy and honor her father's legacy. The path ahead was uncertain and filled with challenges, but Liora was determined to walk it with courage, wisdom, and an unbreakable spirit.

Chapter 6

The discovery of the ancient manuscripts had breathed new life into Liora's studies. With each passing day, she delved deeper into the mysteries of alchemy, her understanding growing alongside her skills. Yet, she knew that the answers she sought—the true secrets of the Essence of Eternity—might lie beyond the texts she had inherited. There was one place she had yet to explore: the hidden laboratory.

Her father had always been secretive about the basement laboratory, forbidding her from entering it when she was a child. Now, with Kael's encouragement and support, Liora felt ready to uncover its secrets. She sensed that it was there that her father had conducted his most profound and dangerous experiments, and she hoped it would hold the key to completing his work.

One morning, after a particularly grueling session of transmutation exercises, Liora approached Kael with her decision.

"I think it's time," she said, her voice steady but filled with anticipation. "I want to explore the hidden laboratory. There might be answers there that we can't find in the manuscripts."

Kael nodded, his expression serious. "I agree. Your father's most important work would have been kept in the safest and most secure place. We need to be prepared for what we might find, though. The laboratory could hold both valuable knowledge and significant dangers."

They spent the rest of the day gathering supplies and preparing for their exploration. Liora felt a mixture of excitement and apprehension, her mind racing with possibilities. She knew that whatever lay in the hidden laboratory would be crucial to her journey, but she also understood that the path ahead could be perilous.

As evening fell, they made their way to the basement. The entrance to the laboratory was concealed behind a heavy bookcase, which Kael helped her move aside. Behind it was a thick wooden door, reinforced with iron bands and secured with a complex lock. Liora examined the lock, recognizing the intricate alchemical symbols etched into its surface.

"This lock is designed to be opened with a specific alchemical key," Kael explained. "Your father must have created it to ensure that only someone with the right knowledge and skill could gain access."

Liora took a deep breath and concentrated. Using the principles she had learned, she carefully crafted an alchemical solution, applying it to the lock. The symbols glowed softly as the solution reacted, and with a satisfying click, the lock disengaged.

Kael pushed the door open, revealing a narrow staircase leading down into darkness. They descended cautiously, the air growing cooler and the shadows deeper with each step. At the bottom of the stairs, they found themselves in a large, cavernous room filled with alchemical apparatuses, shelves of books and ingredients, and a central workbench covered in notes and diagrams.

The laboratory was a testament to her father's brilliance and dedication. Liora felt a surge of pride and sadness, knowing how much effort and sacrifice had gone into his work. She approached the workbench, her eyes scanning the meticulously organized notes.

"Your father was working on something extraordinary," Kael said, his voice filled with awe. "Look at the complexity of these formulas and the depth of his research. He was closer to understanding the Essence of Eternity than anyone in centuries."

Liora nodded, her fingers tracing the lines of a detailed diagram. "He believed in the potential of alchemy to transform not just materials, but the very essence of life.

These notes... they're a culmination of his life's work. I have to continue it."

As they examined the laboratory, they found several completed elixirs and transmuted materials, each one a marvel of alchemical ingenuity. There were vials of glowing liquids, metals that shimmered with an inner light, and crystals that pulsed with elemental energy.

Liora's attention was drawn to a large, leather-bound journal lying open on the workbench. It was her father's personal research journal, filled with his thoughts, observations, and insights. She began reading, her heart pounding with excitement as she absorbed his words.

"My dear Liora," the journal began, "if you are reading this, it means you have found the laboratory and are ready to continue my work. The journey you are about to undertake is fraught with challenges and dangers, but I believe in your strength and wisdom. The Essence of Eternity is not just an elixir—it is the culmination of our understanding of alchemy, a harmony between the alchemist and the elements. To complete it, you must unlock the secrets of the elements and understand the true nature of transformation."

Liora felt a surge of determination. Her father had believed in her, and she was determined to honor his legacy. She continued reading, absorbing his detailed notes on the Essence of Eternity and the steps required to complete the formula.

As she read, she realized that the key to the Essence of Eternity lay in a series of elemental infusions, each one more complex and powerful than the last. Her father had identified the necessary ingredients and processes, but he had not been able to complete the final infusion.

"We need to gather the rare ingredients and perform the elemental infusions," Liora said, her voice filled with resolve. "My father has outlined the steps, but it will require precise control and a deep understanding of the elements."

Kael nodded, his expression serious. "We'll need to prepare carefully and proceed with caution. The final infusion will be incredibly powerful and potentially dangerous. But I believe you have the skill and determination to succeed."

Over the next few weeks, Liora and Kael dedicated themselves to gathering the rare ingredients and perfecting the elemental infusions. They traveled to distant lands, seeking out ancient herbs, magical minerals, and elemental essences. Each journey brought new challenges, testing their abilities and their resolve.

During one such expedition, they ventured into the heart of an ancient forest, seeking a rare flower known as the Moon's Tear. According to her father's notes, the flower bloomed only under the light of a full moon and contained a powerful elemental essence.

The forest was thick and tangled, filled with hidden dangers and mystical creatures. As they made their way deeper into the woods, Liora felt a growing sense of connection to the natural world. She could sense the elemental energies pulsing through the trees, the earth, and the air.

On the night of the full moon, they found a secluded glade where the Moon's Tear was said to bloom. The flower's delicate petals glowed with a silvery light, its essence resonating with the power of the moon. Liora approached it reverently, feeling the energy course through her as she carefully harvested the flower.

With each ingredient they gathered, Liora felt her understanding of alchemy deepen. She learned to harmonize with the elements, to channel their energies with precision and intent. Kael's guidance was invaluable, his knowledge and experience helping her navigate the complexities of the infusions.

Back in the laboratory, they began the process of performing the elemental infusions. Each step required meticulous preparation and flawless execution. Liora worked tirelessly, her focus unwavering as she combined the ingredients and channeled the elemental energies.

The final infusion was the most challenging. It required the essence of all four elements—earth, water, fire, and air—combined in perfect harmony. Liora and Kael prepared carefully, knowing that any mistake could have catastrophic consequences.

As they began the infusion, Liora felt the elemental energies converge, a powerful force that pulsed through her. She focused her mind, channeling the energies with precision and intent. The process was intense, pushing her to the limits of her abilities.

Finally, with a surge of energy, the infusion was complete. The result was a radiant elixir, its essence glowing with the combined power of the elements. Liora held the vial in her hands, feeling a profound sense of accomplishment and fulfillment.

Kael smiled, his eyes filled with pride. "You've done it, Liora. You've completed the final infusion. This elixir represents the true potential of alchemy, a harmony between the alchemist and the elements."

Liora felt a deep sense of connection to her father and to the ancient alchemists who had come before her. She had unlocked the secrets of the Essence of Eternity, fulfilling her father's legacy and discovering her own true potential.

As they stood in the laboratory, surrounded by the fruits of their labor, Liora knew that her journey was far from over. There were still many mysteries to unravel, many challenges to face. But with Kael by her side and the wisdom of her father guiding her, she felt ready to face whatever lay ahead.

The hidden laboratory had revealed its secrets, but it was just the beginning. Liora's journey into the heart of alchemy was a path of endless discovery and transformation, a journey that she was determined to walk with courage, wisdom, and an unbreakable spirit.

Chapter 7

With the completion of the final infusion, Liora felt a surge of confidence and determination. The Essence of Eternity was a testament to her growth as an alchemist, but it also marked the beginning of a new chapter in her journey. As she and Kael continued their studies and experiments, a sense of urgency began to take hold. The political landscape of Althea was becoming increasingly unstable, and rumors of war were spreading like wildfire.

One morning, as Liora and Kael were preparing for another day of study, a messenger arrived at the manor. He was a young man, breathless and covered in dust from his journey. He handed Liora a sealed letter, his expression grave.

"This is from the Council of Elders," the messenger said. "They request your presence in Elaria immediately. It's urgent."

Liora exchanged a worried glance with Kael before breaking the seal and reading the letter. The Council of Elders, the governing body of Althea, had summoned her to discuss a matter of great importance. The letter hinted at rising tensions between neighboring kingdoms and the potential for conflict.

"We should leave at once," Kael said, his voice firm. "The Council wouldn't summon you without a significant reason. We must be prepared for whatever they need."

Liora nodded, feeling a knot of anxiety form in her stomach. She quickly gathered her things, securing the essential alchemical texts and ingredients she might need. Within the hour, they were on the road to Elaria, the capital city of Althea.

The journey was tense and quiet, the weight of the unknown pressing down on them. As they approached Elaria, the city's towering walls and bustling streets came into view. The capital was a stark contrast to the peaceful solitude of the manor, its energy vibrant and chaotic.

At the Council Hall, Liora and Kael were ushered into a grand chamber where the Elders were gathered. The room was filled with an air of solemnity, the faces of the Elders grave and concerned.

"Thank you for coming so quickly, Liora," Elder Thane said, a wise and respected leader among them. "We are facing a crisis, and we need your help."

Liora took a deep breath, steadying herself. "What's happening, Elder Thane?"

Thane's expression was grim. "Tensions between Althea and the neighboring kingdom of Volantis have reached a boiling point. There have been skirmishes along the border, and it's only a matter of time before it escalates into full-scale war. We have reason to believe that Volantis is seeking powerful alchemical weapons to tip the balance in their favor."

Liora's heart sank. The thought of her beloved alchemy being used for destruction was abhorrent to her. "What do you need me to do?"

"We need you to use your knowledge and skills to create defensive measures," Thane replied. "Althea must be prepared to protect itself if war comes. Your father's legacy and your own talents could be the key to ensuring our survival."

Liora felt a surge of determination. She had always believed in the potential of alchemy to transform and heal, but now she was being called upon to use it for protection. It was a daunting task, but one she was willing to undertake.

"I will do whatever I can to help," she said, her voice resolute.

Kael placed a reassuring hand on her shoulder. "We will need to return to the manor to prepare. There is much work to be done."

The Elders nodded, their expressions a mixture of relief and gratitude. "Thank you, Liora," Thane said. "We have faith in you."

As Liora and Kael made their way back to the manor, the weight of their mission settled heavily on their shoulders. They discussed strategies and ideas, brainstorming ways to use alchemy for defense without compromising its core principles.

Back at the manor, they set to work immediately. Liora focused on creating protective elixirs and charms, drawing on her extensive knowledge of elemental infusion. Kael, with his background in martial alchemy, developed alchemical weapons and barriers that could be used to safeguard Althea's borders.

Days turned into weeks as they worked tirelessly, their efforts fueled by a sense of urgency and purpose. The laboratory became a hive of activity, filled with the hum of alchemical processes and the glow of transmuted materials.

One evening, as Liora was refining a particularly complex elixir, Kael approached her with a concerned expression. "Liora, I've been hearing troubling reports from our allies along the border. It seems that Volantis has already acquired some powerful alchemical weapons. We need to accelerate our efforts."

Liora nodded, feeling a surge of anxiety. The threat was growing, and time was running out. She pushed herself harder, working late into the night to perfect her formulas and ensure their effectiveness.

Despite the mounting pressure, Liora and Kael found moments of solace in their shared dedication and mutual support. Their bond grew stronger, their partnership evolving into a deep and unspoken understanding. They were united in their mission, driven by a common goal to protect their homeland.

As the defensive measures took shape, Liora felt a growing sense of hope. They were making progress, creating powerful tools to safeguard Althea. But the looming threat of war cast a shadow over their work, a constant reminder of the stakes involved.

One afternoon, as they were testing a new alchemical barrier, a messenger arrived with urgent news. Volantis had launched a surprise attack on a border town, leaving destruction in its wake. The conflict had officially begun.

Liora's heart pounded with a mixture of fear and determination. The time had come to put their preparations to the test. She and Kael gathered their completed defensive measures and set out for the front lines, ready to aid in the defense of Althea.

The journey to the border was fraught with tension. As they neared the conflict zone, the signs of battle became increasingly evident—burned-out buildings, hastily constructed fortifications, and weary soldiers.

Upon their arrival, they were met by Commander Aric, a seasoned warrior who had been leading the defense efforts. His face was lined with fatigue, but his eyes held a steely resolve.

"Thank you for coming," Aric said, his voice gruff but grateful. "We need all the help we can get. Volantis has been relentless, and their alchemical weapons are devastating."

Liora and Kael wasted no time in deploying their defensive measures. Liora distributed her protective elixirs to the soldiers, explaining their use and effects. The elixirs would enhance their strength and resilience, providing an edge in the brutal combat.

Kael worked with the engineers to set up the alchemical barriers, powerful constructs that could repel attacks and shield the defenders. The barriers glowed with elemental energy, a testament to the meticulous work that had gone into their creation.

As night fell, the first wave of Volantis soldiers approached. The defenders braced themselves, their spirits bolstered by the newfound hope provided by Liora and Kael's alchemical defenses.

The battle was fierce and relentless. The night was filled with the clash of weapons, the cries of combatants, and the glow of alchemical energies. Liora moved among the defenders, administering elixirs and providing support wherever she could. Kael fought alongside the soldiers, his martial alchemy skills proving invaluable in the heat of battle.

Despite the chaos and danger, the alchemical defenses held strong. The protective barriers repelled attacks, and the enhanced strength of the defenders turned the tide in their favor. Liora's heart swelled with pride and determination as she witnessed the effectiveness of their efforts.

As dawn broke, the Volantis forces began to retreat, their momentum broken by the steadfast defense of Althea's soldiers. The battle had been won, but the war was far from over.

Liora and Kael took a moment to catch their breath, the exhaustion of the night's events weighing heavily on them. Commander Aric approached, his expression a mixture of relief and gratitude.

"You've done a remarkable job," Aric said, his voice filled with admiration. "Your alchemical defenses were the key to our victory. We owe you a great debt."

Liora nodded, feeling a deep sense of fulfillment. "We're not done yet," she said, her voice resolute. "There is still much to do. We need to strengthen our defenses and prepare for the next battle."

Kael placed a reassuring hand on her shoulder. "We'll face whatever comes together. Althea will not fall while we stand to protect it."

As they looked out over the battlefield, Liora felt a renewed sense of purpose. The growing threat of Volantis had brought out the best in her, challenging her to rise to the occasion and fulfill her father's legacy. With Kael by her side and the support of Althea's defenders, she was ready to face whatever challenges lay ahead.

The path of the alchemist was one of transformation and enlightenment, but it was also a path of courage and sacrifice. Liora knew that the journey was far from over, but she was determined to walk it with unwavering resolve and an unbreakable spirit. The future of Althea depended on it.

Chapter 8

The victory at the border had bolstered the morale of Althea's defenders, but the threat from Volantis was far from over. Liora and Kael knew that the enemy would regroup and return with even greater force. They redoubled their efforts, working tirelessly to strengthen Althea's defenses and prepare for the next assault.

One afternoon, as Liora and Kael were reviewing the latest reports from the front lines, a messenger arrived with urgent news. Commander Aric had requested their presence at a strategic meeting in Elaria. The situation was becoming increasingly dire, and they needed to coordinate their efforts to protect the kingdom.

Liora and Kael set out for Elaria immediately, their minds focused on the task ahead. The journey was swift and uneventful, but a sense of foreboding hung over them. They arrived at the Council Hall to find the atmosphere tense and strained.

Commander Aric greeted them with a grim expression. "Thank you for coming so quickly," he said. "We've received intelligence that Volantis is planning a major offensive. They've been amassing troops and alchemical weapons. We need to prepare for the worst."

Liora felt a knot of anxiety in her stomach. The stakes were higher than ever, and the fate of Althea hung in the balance. "What can we do to help?" she asked, her voice steady despite the fear gnawing at her.

"We need to reinforce our defenses and ensure that our troops are well-equipped," Aric replied. "Your alchemical expertise will be crucial. We also need to uncover any information about Volantis' plans and neutralize any threats from within."

Liora and Kael nodded, determined to do whatever it took to protect their homeland. They spent the next few days working closely with the military leaders, refining their defensive strategies and preparing for the impending attack.

One evening, as Liora was reviewing a list of supplies, she noticed a shadowy figure lingering near the Council Hall. Her instincts told her that something was amiss. She discreetly followed the figure, keeping to the shadows as she trailed them through the winding streets of Elaria.

The figure led her to a secluded alley, where they met with another person. Liora strained to hear their conversation, her heart pounding with anticipation.

"The Council is planning a major counterattack," the first figure said, their voice low and urgent. "We need to get this information to Volantis immediately."

Liora's blood ran cold. A spy within their ranks was feeding information to the enemy. She had to act quickly to prevent the betrayal from endangering Althea's defenses. She carefully backed away from the alley and hurried back to the Council Hall.

"Kael, we have a problem," she said, finding him in the strategy room. "I just overheard a conversation. There's a spy among us, and they're passing information to Volantis."

Kael's expression hardened. "We need to inform Commander Aric immediately and track down the traitor. This could jeopardize everything we've worked for."

They quickly found Aric and relayed what Liora had overheard. The commander's face darkened with anger and determination. "We must root out this traitor and stop them before they can do any more damage. Liora, Kael, I need you to help with the investigation. We'll tighten security and question anyone who might be involved."

Liora and Kael set to work, interviewing members of the Council and cross-referencing their movements. It was a painstaking process, but their determination fueled their efforts. They knew that the safety of Althea depended on uncovering the spy and preventing further betrayal.

As they delved deeper into the investigation, they began to uncover a web of deceit and treachery. It became clear that the spy had been operating for some time, feeding crucial information to Volantis and undermining Althea's defenses from within.

One night, as they were poring over the evidence, Kael's face grew pale. "Liora, look at this," he said, pointing to a series of notes. "These correspondences match the handwriting of someone we trusted."

Liora's heart sank as she recognized the handwriting. It belonged to one of their close allies, someone who had been instrumental in their efforts to protect Althea. The realization felt like a punch to the gut. Betrayal had come from within their own ranks.

"We need to confront them," Kael said, his voice tight with anger. "They must be stopped before they can do any more harm."

They approached the traitor cautiously, knowing that any confrontation could turn dangerous. When they revealed what they had discovered, the traitor's face twisted with fear and desperation.

"I had no choice," the traitor pleaded. "Volantis threatened my family. They forced me to give them information. I never wanted to betray Althea."

Liora's heart ached with a mix of anger and pity. "You've endangered countless lives," she said, her voice trembling. "Your actions have put all of Althea at risk."

Before they could take the traitor into custody, a sudden commotion erupted outside. A group of Volantis soldiers, tipped off by the spy, had launched a surprise attack on the Council Hall. The situation devolved into chaos as the defenders scrambled to repel the invaders.

In the ensuing battle, Liora and Kael fought side by side, their skills and determination tested to the limit. The traitor, driven by guilt and desperation, joined the fight, trying to atone for their betrayal. But the odds were against them, and the battle took a heavy toll.

Liora felt a searing pain as an enemy blade cut through her side. She staggered, her vision blurring with pain. Kael rushed to her side, his face etched with concern.

"We need to get you out of here," he said, his voice urgent. "You're hurt."

Liora shook her head, determined to continue fighting. "We can't abandon the others. We have to protect the Council."

With Kael's support, Liora continued to fight, drawing on her remaining strength and the power of her alchemical elixirs. Together, they managed to repel the attackers, but the cost was high. Many defenders lay wounded or dead, and the Council Hall was left in ruins.

As the dust settled, Liora and Kael found the traitor among the fallen, their life slipping away. The traitor's eyes were filled with regret and sorrow.

"I'm sorry," the traitor whispered, their voice weak. "I never wanted this. Please forgive me."

Liora felt a pang of sadness. Despite the betrayal, she could see the humanity in the traitor's eyes. "Rest now," she said softly. "Your suffering is over."

The loss weighed heavily on Liora's heart. The battle had been a stark reminder of the fragility of trust and the high cost of betrayal. As she and Kael tended to the wounded and assessed the damage, she knew that the road ahead would be even more challenging.

"We need to stay vigilant," Kael said, his voice filled with resolve. "The threat from Volantis is growing, and we can't afford to let our guard down."

Liora nodded, her determination unwavering. "We'll protect Althea, no matter the cost. We owe it to those who have fallen, and to everyone who depends on us."

As they stood together in the aftermath of the battle, Liora felt a renewed sense of purpose. The path of the alchemist was one of transformation and enlightenment, but it was also a path of courage and sacrifice. With Kael by her side and the memory of those they had lost driving her forward, she was ready to face whatever challenges lay ahead.

The betrayal and loss had left a deep mark on Liora's heart, but it had also strengthened her resolve. She would honor her father's legacy and protect her homeland with every ounce of her strength. The journey was far from over, but Liora knew that she was ready to walk it with courage, wisdom, and an unbreakable spirit. The future of Althea depended on it.

Chapter 9

The battle at the Council Hall had taken its toll on Althea's defenders, but it had also strengthened their resolve. Liora and Kael knew that the fight against Volantis was far from over, and they needed to regroup, rebuild, and prepare for the next assault. The immediate threat had been repelled, but the looming shadow of war still hung over the kingdom.

With the traitor identified and neutralized, Liora and Kael turned their attention to bolstering Althea's defenses and seeking new allies. They knew that the key to victory lay not only in alchemical prowess but also in unity and strategic alliances. They decided to reach out to the scattered remnants of the alchemist guilds, hoping to gather support and resources for the battles ahead.

One morning, as they were preparing to leave for their journey, Commander Aric approached them with a map and a list of contacts. "These are the locations of the remaining alchemist guilds and potential allies," he said.

"We need to forge alliances and gather as much support as possible. The more united we are, the stronger we will be against Volantis."

Liora and Kael set out on their journey, traveling across the kingdom to meet with the alchemists and leaders who might be willing to join their cause. The road was long and fraught with challenges, but their determination never wavered.

Their first destination was the town of Arondale, where a small but respected alchemist guild was based. The guild leader, Master Alaric, was known for his wisdom and knowledge of ancient alchemical practices. Liora and Kael hoped to gain his support and learn from his expertise.

Upon arriving in Arondale, they found the guildhall bustling with activity. Alchemists of all ages were working diligently, their faces etched with concentration and determination. Master Alaric greeted them warmly, his eyes twinkling with curiosity.

"Welcome, Liora and Kael," he said, his voice rich with experience. "I've heard of your efforts and the battles you've fought. What brings you to Arondale?"

Liora explained their mission, detailing the threat from Volantis and the need for unity among the alchemists of Althea. "We seek your guidance and support, Master Alaric," she said earnestly. "We need to stand together to protect our kingdom."

Alaric listened intently, his expression thoughtful. "You speak with passion and conviction, Liora. I can see why your father held you in such high regard. The threat you describe is grave, and it is clear that we must act."

He turned to the members of his guild. "We will join forces with Liora and Kael. Together, we will use our knowledge and skills to protect Althea. Prepare for departure, for we have much work to do."

The alchemists of Arondale quickly mobilized, gathering supplies and preparing to travel to Elaria. Liora and Kael were grateful for their support, knowing that Master Alaric's wisdom and the skills of his guild would be invaluable in the fight against Volantis.

Their next stop was the coastal city of Lythor, where another influential alchemist guild resided. The journey was arduous, with rough terrain and unpredictable weather slowing their progress. Along the way, they encountered bandits and hostile creatures, testing their resolve and abilities.

One evening, as they camped by a river, they were ambushed by a group of mercenaries hired by Volantis. The attackers were skilled and ruthless, seeking to eliminate Liora and Kael before they could gather more allies. The battle was fierce, but Liora and Kael fought with unwavering determination, using their alchemical skills to overcome the odds.

In the heat of the battle, Liora felt a surge of energy, her connection to the elements intensifying. She channeled the power of fire, creating a barrier of flames that drove the mercenaries back. Kael, wielding his martial alchemy with precision, took down their leader, sending the remaining attackers fleeing into the night.

As they caught their breath and tended to their wounds, Liora and Kael realized the true extent of the threat they faced. Volantis would stop at nothing to prevent them from uniting the alchemist guilds and strengthening Althea's defenses.

"We must stay vigilant," Kael said, his voice resolute. "They will keep coming for us, trying to stop us at every turn. But we can't let them succeed. We have to keep moving forward."

Liora nodded, her determination unwavering. "We'll face whatever comes our way, Kael. Together, we'll protect Althea and honor my father's legacy."

They continued their journey, arriving in Lythor a few days later. The city was bustling with activity, its port filled with ships and traders from distant lands. The alchemist guild of Lythor, led by Mistress Elara, was renowned for its maritime alchemy and expertise in healing elixirs.

Mistress Elara greeted them with a warm smile, her presence commanding and reassuring. "Welcome, Liora and Kael. I've heard much about your efforts. What brings you to Lythor?"

Liora explained their mission, emphasizing the importance of unity and collaboration in the face of the growing threat from Volantis. "We need your support, Mistress Elara," she said earnestly. "Together, we can protect our kingdom and ensure a future of peace and prosperity."

Elara listened carefully, her eyes reflecting a deep understanding. "You are wise beyond your years, Liora. The threat from Volantis is indeed serious, and we must stand together to face it. The alchemists of Lythor will join your cause."

The members of Elara's guild began preparing for their journey to Elaria, their spirits lifted by the prospect of contributing to the defense of their homeland. Liora and Kael felt a renewed sense of hope, knowing that the support of Lythor's alchemists would greatly strengthen their efforts.

As they traveled back to Elaria with their newfound allies, Liora and Kael encountered other groups of alchemists and defenders who pledged their support. The journey was long and challenging, but their determination and unity never wavered.

Upon their return to Elaria, they were greeted with a mixture of relief and celebration. The presence of the alchemist guilds from Arondale and Lythor brought a new sense of hope and strength to the defenders of Althea. The city buzzed with activity as preparations for the next battle intensified.

Commander Aric welcomed them back with open arms, his face etched with gratitude. "Your efforts have brought us valuable allies and resources. We are stronger now, thanks to you. But the fight is far from over."

Liora and Kael knew that the road ahead would be difficult, but they were ready to face whatever challenges lay ahead. They continued to work tirelessly, refining their alchemical defenses and training the defenders in new techniques and strategies.

One evening, as they were discussing their plans, a messenger arrived with urgent news. Volantis had launched another attack, this time targeting a key stronghold on the eastern border. The situation was dire, and the defenders were struggling to hold their ground.

"We must go to their aid," Liora said, her voice filled with determination. "We can't let Volantis gain any more ground."

Kael nodded, his expression resolute. "We'll gather our allies and head to the eastern stronghold. We must protect it at all costs."

As they prepared to leave, Liora felt a sense of unity and purpose that bolstered her spirits. The alliances they had forged and the support of their fellow alchemists gave her hope that they could overcome the darkness that threatened their kingdom.

The journey to the eastern stronghold was swift and intense, their determination driving them forward. As they arrived, they saw the signs of battle—smoke rising from the fortifications, the clash of weapons echoing through the air.

Liora and Kael quickly joined the fray, their alchemical skills turning the tide of the battle. The defenders, inspired by their presence and the support of the allied alchemists, fought with renewed vigor and determination.

The battle was fierce and unrelenting, but Liora and Kael's leadership and alchemical prowess made a significant difference. They coordinated the efforts of the defenders, using their knowledge of alchemy to create powerful defenses and strategic advantages.

As the sun set and the battle raged on, Liora felt a surge of energy and determination. She knew that the fight for Althea's future was far from over, but she was ready to face whatever challenges lay ahead. With Kael by her side and the support of their allies, she was confident that they could protect their homeland and ensure a future of peace and prosperity.

The path of the alchemist was one of transformation and enlightenment, but it was also a path of courage, sacrifice, and unity. Liora knew that her journey was far from over, but she was determined to walk it with unwavering resolve and an unbreakable spirit. The future of Althea depended on it.

Chapter 10

The eastern stronghold had been secured, but the respite was brief. Volantis, undeterred by their defeat, was amassing its forces for a full-scale invasion of Althea. The air was thick with tension as the defenders braced for the inevitable clash. Liora and Kael knew that the coming days would test their resolve, strength, and the very essence of their alchemical abilities.

Back in Elaria, the atmosphere was one of urgent preparation. The streets buzzed with activity as soldiers armed themselves and alchemists brewed potent elixirs. The Council Hall had become a war room, filled with maps, strategies, and the determined faces of those ready to defend their homeland.

Liora and Kael were at the heart of the preparations, their expertise and leadership crucial in coordinating the defense. As they stood over a map of Althea, discussing strategies with Commander Aric, the gravity of the situation weighed heavily on them.

"Volantis is advancing from multiple fronts," Aric said, tracing the enemy's movements on the map. "Their forces are vast, and their use of alchemical weapons is unlike anything we've seen. We must hold our ground here, at the central valley. It's the key to defending Elaria and the rest of the kingdom."

Liora nodded, her mind racing with possibilities. "We need to use the terrain to our advantage. If we can funnel their forces into the valley, we can create choke points and use our alchemical defenses to repel them."

Kael added, "We should also set up ambushes along the forest paths. Our allies from Arondale and Lythor can create traps and barriers to slow their advance. The element of surprise will be crucial."

Aric agreed, and they spent the next few hours refining their plans, assigning tasks, and rallying the defenders. Liora and Kael worked tirelessly, their determination and resolve never wavering. They knew that the fate of Althea rested on their shoulders.

As the sun set, casting a golden glow over Elaria, Liora took a moment to reflect. She stood on a balcony overlooking the city, the weight of the coming battle pressing down on her. The memories of her father, her journey, and the sacrifices made along the way filled her thoughts.

Kael joined her, his presence a comforting anchor. "We've come a long way, Liora," he said softly. "No matter what happens, know that you've made a difference. Your father would be proud."

Liora took a deep breath, finding strength in his words. "We'll protect Althea, Kael. We'll honor my father's legacy and ensure a future for our people."

The next morning, the defenders of Althea assembled in the central valley, ready to face the advancing forces of Volantis. The atmosphere was charged with anticipation and determination. Liora and Kael moved among the troops, offering words of encouragement and distributing the elixirs and weapons they had prepared.

As the first rays of dawn broke over the horizon, the distant rumble of marching feet and clanking armor grew louder. The enemy was approaching. Liora felt a surge of adrenaline, her senses heightened and her mind focused.

The battle began with a deafening roar as the forces of Volantis clashed with the defenders of Althea. The valley echoed with the sounds of combat, the clash of swords, and the cries of warriors. Liora and Kael were at the forefront, their alchemical prowess turning the tide in favor of their allies.

Liora used her elemental infusions to create barriers of fire and ice, repelling the enemy's advances and protecting her comrades. Her movements were fluid and precise, each action a testament to her training and determination. Kael, wielding his martial alchemy with unmatched skill, fought alongside her, their synergy creating a formidable force on the battlefield.

Despite their efforts, the enemy was relentless. Volantis had brought their most powerful alchemists and warriors, and their attacks were fierce and coordinated. The defenders of Althea fought valiantly, but the sheer number of enemies threatened to overwhelm them.

As the battle raged on, Liora spotted a group of enemy alchemists attempting to breach their defenses with a powerful alchemical device. She knew that if they succeeded, it could spell disaster for Althea's forces. Determined to stop them, she called out to Kael.

"We need to take out that device," she shouted over the din of battle. "It's too dangerous to let it reach our lines."

Kael nodded, his expression resolute. "I'll cover you. Let's move."

Together, they fought their way through the chaos, their movements synchronized and purposeful. The enemy alchemists, realizing their intent, tried to intercept them, but Liora and Kael were unstoppable. They reached the device, a complex contraption glowing with ominous energy.

Liora quickly assessed the situation, her mind racing. "We need to disrupt the energy flow. I'll use an elemental infusion to overload it. Keep them off me."

Kael positioned himself between Liora and the enemy, his blades flashing as he defended her from incoming attacks. Liora concentrated, channeling her energy into the infusion. The device began to crackle and spark, its stability wavering.

With a final surge of power, Liora completed the infusion. The device exploded in a brilliant flash of light, sending a shockwave through the battlefield. The enemy alchemists were thrown back, their formation shattered.

Liora and Kael took advantage of the chaos, rallying their allies and pressing the attack. The defenders of Althea, inspired by their leaders' bravery, fought with renewed vigor. The tide of the battle began to turn in their favor.

As the sun reached its zenith, the enemy forces began to falter. The defenders of Althea, bolstered by their alchemical defenses and unwavering determination, pushed them back. The battlefield was a testament to the fierce struggle, but the resolve of Althea's defenders shone through.

By dusk, the remaining forces of Volantis retreated, their assault broken. The defenders of Althea stood victorious, their spirits lifted by the hard-fought victory. The valley, once a place of conflict, now stood as a symbol of their resilience and strength.

Liora and Kael, exhausted but triumphant, surveyed the aftermath. The cost had been high, but their efforts had saved countless lives and secured a crucial victory for Althea.

Commander Aric approached them, his face lined with fatigue but filled with pride. "You've done it," he said, his voice filled with gratitude. "Your leadership and alchemical prowess turned the tide of the battle. Althea owes you a great debt."

Liora shook her head, her gaze steady. "We did it together, Commander. Every defender here played a part. We'll continue to stand united and protect our homeland."

Kael nodded in agreement. "This is just the beginning. We've shown that we can stand against Volantis, but we must remain vigilant. The fight is far from over."

As night fell, the defenders of Althea began the somber task of tending to the wounded and honoring the fallen. The victory was bittersweet, a reminder of the sacrifices made in the name of freedom and peace.

Liora and Kael took a moment to reflect on the day's events. They stood together, their bond stronger than ever, their determination unwavering. The war had begun, but they were ready to face whatever challenges lay ahead.

With the memory of those they had lost driving them forward, Liora and Kael vowed to continue their fight. They would protect Althea, honor their legacy, and ensure a future of peace and prosperity. The path of the alchemist was one of transformation and enlightenment, but it was also a path of courage, sacrifice, and unity.

The future of Althea depended on it, and Liora was determined to see it through, no matter the cost. The journey was far from over, but with Kael by her side and the support of their allies, she knew they could overcome any obstacle and achieve a brighter future for their kingdom.

Chapter 11

The victory in the central valley had given Althea a much-needed respite, but the threat from Volantis loomed large. Liora and Kael knew that the battle was only the beginning of a long and arduous war. As they continued to fortify their defenses and strategize for the next confrontation, Liora found herself drawn to her father's journals and the secrets they might still hold.

One evening, after a long day of planning and preparation, Liora retreated to her father's study. The room was a sanctuary of memories and knowledge, filled with the scent of old parchment and the faint hum of alchemical energy. She sat at the large oak desk, her fingers tracing the worn leather cover of her father's journal.

Kael entered the study, his presence a comforting anchor. "You've been spending a lot of time in here," he said softly. "What's on your mind, Liora?"

Liora sighed, her eyes lingering on the pages of the journal. "I can't shake the feeling that there's more to my father's work than we've uncovered. His notes, his experiments—they all point to something deeper. I need to understand his true purpose."

Kael nodded, his expression thoughtful. "Your father was a brilliant alchemist, always searching for knowledge and understanding. If there are secrets hidden in his work, we'll find them together."

Determined to uncover the truth, Liora delved into her father's journals, her mind racing with questions and possibilities. She read through his meticulous notes, tracing the evolution of his research and the insights he had gained. As she pieced together the fragments of his work, a pattern began to emerge.

One entry in particular caught her attention. It detailed a series of experiments involving a rare and powerful alchemical artifact known as the Philosopher's Stone. According to her father's notes, the stone had the potential to unlock the secrets of life and death, to transform matter and energy in ways that defied conventional understanding.

Liora's heart pounded with excitement. The Philosopher's Stone was a legendary artifact, believed to be a myth by many. If her father had discovered its existence and potential, it could explain the depths of his research and the risks he had taken.

As she read further, she found references to a hidden chamber beneath the manor, a place where her father had conducted his most secret and profound experiments. The chamber was protected by powerful alchemical wards, designed to keep it hidden and secure.

"Kael, look at this," Liora said, her voice filled with awe. "My father was researching the Philosopher's Stone. He mentioned a hidden chamber beneath the manor where he conducted his experiments. We need to find it."

Kael's eyes widened with interest. "The Philosopher's Stone? If your father was studying it, that could be the key to understanding his work and its true purpose. Let's find that chamber."

Guided by her father's notes, Liora and Kael searched the manor for any clues that might lead them to the hidden chamber. They examined every corner, every hidden passage, until they discovered a concealed door in the basement, covered in alchemical symbols and runes.

Liora carefully deciphered the symbols, her mind focused and determined. She applied a series of alchemical solutions to the door, unlocking its complex mechanisms. With a final click, the door swung open, revealing a staircase descending into darkness.

Taking a deep breath, Liora and Kael descended the stairs, their steps echoing in the silence. The air grew cooler as they ventured deeper, the walls lined with ancient stone. At the bottom of the staircase, they found themselves in a vast underground chamber, filled with alchemical apparatuses, shelves of rare ingredients, and a central workbench covered in intricate notes and diagrams.

The chamber was a testament to her father's brilliance and dedication. Liora felt a surge of pride and sadness, knowing how much he had sacrificed in his pursuit of knowledge. She approached the workbench, her eyes scanning the meticulously organized notes.

"These are his most advanced experiments," Kael said, his voice filled with awe. "Look at the complexity of these formulas and the depth of his research. He was closer to understanding the Philosopher's Stone than anyone in centuries."

Liora nodded, her fingers tracing the lines of a detailed diagram. "He believed in the potential of the stone to transform not just materials, but the very essence of life. These notes... they're a culmination of his life's work. I have to continue it."

As they examined the chamber, they found several completed elixirs and transmuted materials, each one a marvel of alchemical ingenuity. There were vials of glowing liquids, metals that shimmered with an inner light, and crystals that pulsed with elemental energy.

Liora's attention was drawn to a large, leather-bound journal lying open on the workbench. It was her father's personal research journal, filled with his thoughts, observations, and insights. She began reading, her heart pounding with excitement as she absorbed his words.

"My dear Liora," the journal began, "if you are reading this, it means you have found the hidden chamber and are ready to continue my work. The Philosopher's Stone is not just a legend—it is real, and it holds the key to unlocking the true potential of alchemy. But its power is both immense and dangerous. To wield it, one must understand the balance between creation and destruction, between life and death."

Liora felt a surge of determination. Her father had believed in her, and she was determined to honor his legacy. She continued reading, absorbing his detailed notes on the Philosopher's Stone and the steps required to complete his research.

As she read, she realized that the key to unlocking the stone's potential lay in a series of elemental infusions, each one more complex and powerful than the last. Her father had identified the necessary ingredients and processes, but he had not been able to complete the final infusion.

"We need to gather the rare ingredients and perform the elemental infusions," Liora said, her voice filled with resolve. "My father has outlined the steps, but it will require precise control and a deep understanding of the elements."

Kael nodded, his expression serious. "We'll need to prepare carefully and proceed with caution. The final infusion will be incredibly powerful and potentially dangerous. But I believe you have the skill and determination to succeed."

Over the next few weeks, Liora and Kael dedicated themselves to gathering the rare ingredients and perfecting the elemental infusions. They traveled to distant lands, seeking out ancient herbs, magical minerals, and elemental essences. Each journey brought new challenges, testing their abilities and their resolve.

During one such expedition, they ventured into the heart of an ancient forest, seeking a rare flower known as the Moon's Tear. According to her father's notes, the flower bloomed only under the light of a full moon and contained a powerful elemental essence.

The forest was thick and tangled, filled with hidden dangers and mystical creatures. As they made their way deeper into the woods, Liora felt a growing sense of connection to the natural world. She could sense the elemental energies pulsing through the trees, the earth, and the air.

On the night of the full moon, they found a secluded glade where the Moon's Tear was said to bloom. The flower's delicate petals glowed with a silvery light, its essence resonating with the power of the moon. Liora approached it reverently, feeling the energy course through her as she carefully harvested the flower.

With each ingredient they gathered, Liora felt her understanding of alchemy deepen. She learned to harmonize with the elements, to channel their energies with precision and intent. Kael's guidance was invaluable, his knowledge and experience helping her navigate the complexities of the infusions.

Back in the hidden chamber, they began the process of performing the elemental infusions. Each step required meticulous preparation and flawless execution. Liora worked tirelessly, her focus unwavering as she combined the ingredients and channeled the elemental energies.

The final infusion was the most challenging. It required the essence of all four elements—earth, water, fire, and air—combined in perfect harmony. Liora and Kael prepared carefully, knowing that any mistake could have catastrophic consequences.

As they began the infusion, Liora felt the elemental energies converge, a powerful force that pulsed through her. She focused her mind, channeling the energies with precision and intent. The process was intense, pushing her to the limits of her abilities.

Finally, with a surge of energy, the infusion was complete. The result was a radiant stone, its essence glowing with the combined power of the elements. Liora held the stone in her hands, feeling a profound sense of accomplishment and fulfillment.

Kael smiled, his eyes filled with pride. "You've done it, Liora. You've completed the final infusion. This stone represents the true potential of alchemy, a harmony between the alchemist and the elements."

Liora felt a deep sense of connection to her father and to the ancient alchemists who had come before her. She had unlocked the secrets of the Philosopher's Stone, fulfilling her father's legacy and discovering her own true potential.

As they stood in the hidden chamber, surrounded by the fruits of their labor, Liora knew that her journey was far from over. There were still many mysteries to unravel, many challenges to face. But with Kael by her side and the wisdom of her father guiding her, she felt ready to face whatever lay ahead.

The hidden chamber had revealed its secrets, but it was just the beginning. Liora's journey into the heart of alchemy was a path of endless discovery and transformation, a journey that she was determined to walk with courage, wisdom, and an unbreakable spirit.

Chapter 12

With the Philosopher's Stone in her possession, Liora felt a renewed sense of purpose and determination. The stone represented the culmination of her father's life's work and a powerful tool that could tip the balance in the ongoing war with Volantis. However, its power also brought great responsibility, and Liora knew that she had to use it wisely.

Despite the victory in the central valley, Volantis was far from defeated. Reports of enemy movements and preparations for another major offensive reached Elaria daily. The Council of Elders decided that it was crucial to strike a decisive blow against Volantis, targeting their main alchemical research facility. Destroying it would cripple their ability to produce alchemical weapons and provide a significant advantage to Althea.

The journey to the facility was fraught with peril, located deep within the territory controlled by Volantis. Liora and Kael volunteered for the mission, knowing that their expertise in alchemy and combat would be essential for its success. They assembled a small team of elite soldiers and alchemists, prepared for the dangerous journey ahead.

As they gathered their supplies and prepared to leave, Liora couldn't help but feel a mix of excitement and apprehension. She had come a long way since discovering her father's hidden legacy, and now she stood on the brink of a mission that could determine the fate of her kingdom.

Kael approached her, his expression serious but supportive. "We'll face whatever challenges come our way, Liora. We've trained for this, and we have the support of our allies. Together, we'll succeed."

Liora nodded, feeling reassured by his presence. "I know, Kael. We're ready. Let's do this."

The journey began under the cover of night, their group moving swiftly and silently through the forest. They followed hidden paths and avoided main roads to minimize the risk of detection. The terrain was challenging, but their training and determination kept them moving forward.

After several days of travel, they reached the outskirts of Volantis territory. The air was thick with tension as they scouted the area, searching for a safe route to the alchemical facility. They encountered patrols and traps set by the enemy, forcing them to rely on their skills and ingenuity to avoid detection.

One evening, as they were setting up camp in a secluded grove, Liora and Kael reviewed their plans for the mission. They had identified a hidden entrance to the facility, a network of tunnels used by the enemy for transporting supplies. It would be dangerous, but it offered the best chance of infiltrating the facility undetected.

"We'll need to move quickly and stay alert," Kael said, his eyes scanning the map. "Once we're inside, we can plant the explosives and destroy their equipment. We'll have to be precise and coordinated."

Liora nodded, her mind focused on the task ahead. "We've trained for this. We'll succeed, Kael. For Althea."

As they prepared to rest for the night, a sense of unease settled over the camp. Liora couldn't shake the feeling that they were being watched. She stood on the edge of the camp, her senses heightened, scanning the shadows for any sign of danger.

Kael joined her, sensing her unease. "What is it, Liora?"

"I don't know," she replied, her voice tense. "I just have a feeling that something is off. We need to stay vigilant."

Kael placed a reassuring hand on her shoulder. "We will. We've come too far to be stopped now."

The next morning, they continued their journey, their progress slowed by the need for constant caution. As they neared the entrance to the tunnels, they encountered a group of Volantis soldiers. A fierce battle ensued, testing their skills and resolve.

Liora and Kael fought side by side, their movements synchronized and deadly. The soldiers of Volantis were relentless, but the determination of Althea's defenders was unwavering. With each swing of Kael's blade and each burst of Liora's alchemical power, they pushed back the enemy.

After a grueling fight, they emerged victorious, though not without losses. The cost of the mission weighed heavily on Liora's heart, but she knew that their sacrifices were necessary for the greater good.

They entered the tunnels, the air cool and damp. The walls were lined with alchemical symbols and runes, a testament to the enemy's knowledge and power. Liora led the way, her keen senses guiding them through the labyrinthine passages.

As they moved deeper into the tunnels, they encountered more traps and guards. Each confrontation was a test of their skills and endurance, but they pressed on, driven by their mission and the knowledge of what was at stake.

Finally, they reached the heart of the facility, a vast chamber filled with alchemical apparatuses and equipment. The air hummed with energy, the scent of chemicals and magic thick in the air.

Liora and Kael quickly set to work, planting explosives and sabotaging the equipment. They moved with precision and efficiency, their actions a testament to their training and determination.

As they completed their task, a sudden sound echoed through the chamber. Liora turned to see a group of enemy alchemists entering the room, their eyes filled with anger and determination.

"We've been discovered," Kael said, his voice tense. "We need to hold them off long enough for the explosives to detonate."

Liora nodded, her heart pounding with adrenaline. "We can do this, Kael. Together."

A fierce battle ensued, the chamber filled with the clash of weapons and the crackle of alchemical energy. Liora and Kael fought with everything they had, their movements a blur of skill and power. The enemy alchemists were formidable, but Liora's determination and Kael's unwavering support gave them the edge.

As the fight raged on, the explosives began to detonate, one after another. The chamber shook with the force of the explosions, the enemy's equipment and apparatuses reduced to rubble.

With a final surge of energy, Liora and Kael defeated the last of the enemy alchemists. The chamber was filled with smoke and debris, the air thick with the scent of destruction. They had succeeded, but the cost had been high.

Exhausted but triumphant, they made their way back through the tunnels, their path lit by the glow of the Philosopher's Stone. The journey back to Althea was fraught with danger, but their determination and the knowledge of their victory kept them moving forward.

When they finally returned to Elaria, they were greeted with a mixture of relief and celebration. The destruction of the alchemical facility had dealt a significant blow to Volantis, and the defenders of Althea felt a renewed sense of hope and determination.

Commander Aric greeted them with open arms, his face filled with gratitude and pride. "You've done it," he said, his voice filled with emotion. "Your bravery and determination have given us a fighting chance. Althea owes you a great debt."

Liora shook her head, her gaze steady. "We did it together, Commander. Every defender here played a part. We'll continue to stand united and protect our homeland."

Kael nodded in agreement. "This is just the beginning. We've shown that we can stand against Volantis, but we must remain vigilant. The fight is far from over."

As night fell, Liora and Kael took a moment to reflect on their journey. They had faced incredible challenges and made great sacrifices, but their determination and unity had carried them through.

With the memory of those they had lost driving them forward, Liora and Kael vowed to continue their fight. They would protect Althea, honor their legacy, and ensure a future of peace and prosperity. The path of the alchemist was one of transformation and enlightenment, but it was also a path of courage, sacrifice, and unity.

The future of Althea depended on it, and Liora was determined to see it through, no matter the cost. The journey was far from over, but with Kael by her side and the support of their allies, she knew they could overcome any obstacle and achieve a brighter future for their kingdom.

Chapter 13

The successful mission to destroy the alchemical facility in Volantis had given Althea a much-needed strategic advantage. The defenders of Althea, bolstered by their victory, worked tirelessly to fortify their defenses and prepare for the next phase of the conflict. Amidst the planning and preparation, Liora and Kael found themselves growing even closer, their bond deepening as they navigated the challenges and dangers together.

One evening, as the sun set over Elaria, casting a warm golden glow across the city, Liora and Kael took a rare moment to relax and reflect. They walked through the gardens of the manor, the air filled with the scent of blooming flowers and the soft chirping of evening crickets.

Liora sighed, her mind heavy with thoughts of the battles ahead. "It feels like we've been fighting for so long, Kael. Sometimes I wonder if we'll ever see an end to this war."

Kael looked at her, his eyes filled with understanding and compassion. "We will, Liora. We've come this far, and we'll continue to fight for Althea. But it's important to take moments like this, to remember what we're fighting for and to find strength in each other."

Liora smiled, feeling a warmth spread through her heart. "You're right. I'm grateful to have you by my side, Kael. I couldn't do this without you."

Kael reached out and gently took her hand, his touch reassuring. "And I'm grateful for you, Liora. Together, we're stronger. We've faced so much already, and we'll face whatever comes next, side by side."

As they continued their walk, the conversation turned to lighter topics, and Liora found herself laughing and smiling, the weight of the war momentarily lifted. It was in these quiet moments that she felt the depth of her connection to Kael, a bond that had grown from mutual respect and shared determination into something much deeper.

That night, as they sat by the fireplace, Liora couldn't help but feel a sense of longing. She had spent so much of her life focused on her studies and her father's legacy, never allowing herself to fully explore her own feelings and desires. But with Kael, she felt something different, something she couldn't ignore.

"Kael," she began hesitantly, her voice soft. "I've been thinking about everything we've been through and how much you mean to me. I... I don't want to lose you."

Kael looked at her, his expression tender. "Liora, you mean the world to me. I've felt it too, this connection between us. It's more than just friendship or partnership. It's something deeper."

Liora's heart raced as she reached out and took his hand. "I care about you, Kael. More than I've ever cared about anyone. I don't know what the future holds, but I want to face it with you."

Kael's eyes softened, and he gently cupped her cheek with his hand. "Liora, I feel the same way. I've tried to deny it, to focus on the mission, but I can't ignore my feelings any longer. I love you."

Tears filled Liora's eyes as she leaned into his touch. "I love you too, Kael."

In that moment, the world seemed to fade away, leaving only the two of them. They leaned in, their lips meeting in a tender and passionate kiss. It was a kiss that spoke of all the unspoken words and emotions that had built up between them, a promise of their love and commitment to each other.

As they pulled away, Kael rested his forehead against hers, his breath warm against her skin. "We'll face whatever comes together, Liora. Our love will give us the strength to overcome any obstacle."

Liora nodded, feeling a sense of peace and determination. "Together, Kael. Always."

The next morning, Liora and Kael awoke with a renewed sense of purpose. Their love had given them a new strength, a deeper resolve to protect Althea and create a future where they could be together. They shared their newfound commitment with their closest allies, who greeted the news with joy and support.

As the days turned into weeks, Liora and Kael continued to lead the efforts to fortify Althea's defenses and prepare for the next phase of the war. Their love was a source of inspiration and strength for everyone around them, a beacon of hope in the darkest of times.

One afternoon, as they were working on a complex alchemical defense mechanism, Liora felt a sudden surge of energy. She looked at Kael, her eyes wide with realization. "Kael, I think I've found a way to amplify the Philosopher's Stone's power. It could create a protective barrier around Elaria, strong enough to repel any attack."

Kael's eyes lit up with excitement. "That could change everything, Liora. Let's test it."

They worked together, channeling their combined knowledge and power into the Philosopher's Stone. The process was intense, requiring precise control and co-ordination. As they completed the final steps, the stone began to glow with a brilliant light, its energy radiating outwards.

A shimmering barrier formed around Elaria, its energy pulsing with the combined power of the elements. The defenders of Althea watched in awe as the barrier solidified, creating an impenetrable shield around the city.

"We did it," Liora said, her voice filled with wonder. "We've created a barrier that will protect Elaria."

Kael smiled, his eyes filled with pride. "You did it, Liora. Your brilliance and determination made this possible."

Liora shook her head, her gaze steady. "We did it together, Kael. Our love and partnership made us stronger. This is just the beginning."

The creation of the barrier was a turning point in the war. With Elaria protected, the defenders of Althea had a strategic advantage that allowed them to focus on offensive tactics and further weaken Volantis. The tide of the war began to turn, and hope blossomed among the people of Althea.

As the war continued, Liora and Kael's love grew stronger. They faced each challenge with unwavering resolve, their bond a source of strength and inspiration. Together, they navigated the complexities of alchemy and warfare, always guided by their love and commitment to each other.

One evening, as they stood on the balcony of the manor, watching the sunset, Kael took Liora's hand. "No matter what happens, Liora, I promise to always stand by your side. We'll build a future together, a future filled with love and peace."

Liora's heart swelled with emotion as she looked into his eyes. "And I promise to always be by your side, Kael. Together, we'll create a better world for Althea."

As the sun dipped below the horizon, casting a golden glow across the land, Liora and Kael knew that their journey was far from over. But with their love and determination, they were ready to face whatever challenges lay ahead. The path of the alchemist was one of transformation and enlightenment, and together, they would continue to walk it with courage, wisdom, and an unbreakable spirit.

The future of Althea depended on it, and Liora and Kael were determined to see it through, no matter the cost. With their love as their guiding light, they knew they could overcome any obstacle and achieve a brighter future for their kingdom.

Chapter 14

The protective barrier around Elaria had given the people of Althea hope and a much-needed respite from the relentless attacks by Volantis. Liora and Kael, fueled by their love and the success of their previous endeavors, turned their attention to what might be the most critical task of all: completing the final formula for the Philosopher's Stone. This powerful artifact held the potential to turn the tide of the war once and for all, and Liora was determined to unlock its full potential.

One morning, Liora sat at her father's old desk in the hidden laboratory, surrounded by his meticulous notes and ancient texts. The journal she had discovered earlier, detailing her father's research on the Philosopher's Stone, lay open before her. She had spent countless hours poring over its contents, deciphering the complex alchemical symbols and formulas.

Kael entered the room, his presence a comforting anchor. "How are you feeling, Liora?" he asked, his voice filled with concern and support.

Liora looked up, her eyes reflecting a mix of determination and exhaustion. "I'm close, Kael. I can feel it. The final formula is almost within reach, but there are still a few pieces missing. I need to understand the exact balance of the elemental essences and the catalyst that will activate the stone's full power."

Kael nodded, his expression serious. "We'll find those pieces together. We've come this far, and I believe in you, Liora. Your father's legacy and the future of Althea depend on this."

Liora took a deep breath, drawing strength from Kael's unwavering support. "Thank you, Kael. I couldn't do this without you."

Over the next few days, Liora and Kael worked tirelessly, combining their knowledge and skills to refine the formula. They experimented with various combinations of elemental essences, seeking the perfect balance that would unlock the Philosopher's Stone's true potential.

One evening, as they were deep in their work, Liora had a breakthrough. She realized that the key to the final formula lay in a rare and powerful substance known as Aetherium, an ethereal material that could channel and amplify elemental energies. According to her father's notes, Aetherium could be found in the heart of an ancient, enchanted forest known as the Veilwood.

"We need to find Aetherium," Liora said, her voice filled with excitement and determination. "It's the missing piece of the puzzle. If we can obtain it, we can complete the final formula."

Kael's eyes widened with realization. "The Veilwood is a dangerous place, filled with mystical creatures and ancient magic. But we've faced dangers before, and we can do it again. We need to prepare for the journey."

The next morning, Liora and Kael set out for the Veilwood, accompanied by a small group of trusted allies. The journey was long and arduous, taking them through rugged terrain and treacherous paths. Along the way, they encountered various challenges, including fierce storms, hostile creatures, and difficult terrain. But their determination and the bond they shared kept them moving forward.

As they neared the Veilwood, the atmosphere grew thick with magic. The forest was a place of ancient enchantment, its trees towering high and their leaves shimmering with a silvery light. The air was filled with the whispers of unseen spirits, and the ground seemed to pulse with life.

"We must be cautious," Kael said, his voice low and alert. "The Veilwood is filled with powerful magic and unpredictable dangers. Stay close, and we'll navigate through this together."

Liora nodded, her senses heightened as they entered the enchanted forest. They moved carefully, their eyes scanning the surroundings for any signs of danger or the presence of Aetherium. The forest was a maze of twisted paths and hidden glades, and the sense of otherworldly presence was palpable.

After several days of searching, they reached the heart of the Veilwood, a secluded glade bathed in a soft, ethereal light. In the center of the glade stood a massive, ancient tree with shimmering bark and glowing roots. At the base of the tree, nestled among its roots, was a cluster of radiant crystals—Aetherium.

"We found it," Liora whispered, her voice filled with awe. "This is the Aetherium we need for the final formula."

As they approached the crystals, a group of mystical creatures emerged from the shadows, their eyes filled with curiosity and a hint of warning. They were the guardians of the Veilwood, protectors of the ancient magic that flowed through the forest.

Liora stepped forward, her heart pounding with a mixture of fear and determination. "We seek the Aetherium to protect our homeland and bring peace to Althea. Please, grant us your blessing and allow us to take what we need."

The guardians regarded Liora and her companions with a deep, knowing gaze. After a tense moment, the leader of the guardians stepped forward and nodded. "We sense the purity of your intentions and the strength of your bond. Take the Aetherium, and may it bring you the power you seek."

With the guardians' blessing, Liora carefully harvested the Aetherium, feeling its powerful energy resonate through her. She knew that this was the key to completing the final formula and unlocking the full potential of the Philosopher's Stone.

As they left the Veilwood, Liora and Kael felt a renewed sense of purpose and hope. They returned to Elaria, where they immediately set to work on the final formula. The process was intense, requiring precise control and coordination of the elemental essences and the Aetherium.

For days, they worked tirelessly, channeling their combined knowledge and power into the formula. Liora felt the weight of her father's legacy and the future of Althea on her shoulders, but she also felt the strength of her love for Kael and the support of their allies.

Finally, after countless hours of meticulous work, the final formula was complete. The Philosopher's Stone glowed with a brilliant, radiant light, its energy pulsing with the combined power of the elements and the Aetherium.

"We did it," Liora said, her voice filled with awe and triumph. "The Philosopher's Stone is complete."

Kael smiled, his eyes filled with pride and love. "You did it, Liora. Your brilliance and determination made this possible. Now, we have the power to protect Althea and bring an end to this war."

With the Philosopher's Stone in their possession, Liora and Kael knew that the next step was to use its power wisely. They convened with the Council of Elders and the leaders of Althea's defenses, sharing their success and discussing how to best utilize the stone's immense potential.

As they stood before the gathered leaders, Liora held the Philosopher's Stone high, its light casting a warm glow across the room. "This stone represents the culmination of my father's work and our combined efforts. With its power, we can protect Althea and ensure a future of peace and prosperity."

The leaders of Althea nodded in agreement, their faces filled with hope and determination. "We will use this power to defend our homeland and bring an end to the threat from Volantis. Together, we will achieve victory."

As preparations for the final confrontation with Volantis began, Liora and Kael felt a sense of unity and purpose among the defenders of Althea. The power of the Philosopher's Stone, combined with their love and determination, gave them the strength to face whatever challenges lay ahead.

In the days that followed, Liora and Kael worked tirelessly to harness the power of the Philosopher's Stone, creating powerful alchemical defenses and weapons. The people of Althea, inspired by their leaders' bravery and dedication, rallied together, ready to defend their homeland with all their might.

One evening, as they stood on the balcony of the manor, watching the sun set over Elaria, Liora felt a deep sense of fulfillment and hope. She turned to Kael, her eyes filled with love and determination. "We've come so far, Kael. Together, we've unlocked the true potential of alchemy and forged a bond that will guide us through any challenge."

Kael took her hand, his gaze steady and unwavering. "We'll face whatever comes next, Liora. Our love and the power of the Philosopher's Stone will lead us to victory and a future of peace for Althea."

As the sun dipped below the horizon, casting a golden glow across the land, Liora and Kael knew that their journey was far from over. But with their love and the power of the Philosopher's Stone, they were ready to face whatever challenges lay ahead. The path of the

alchemist was one of transformation and enlightenment, and together, they would continue to walk it with
courage, wisdom, and an unbreakable spirit.

The future of Althea depended on it, and Liora and
Kael were determined to see it through, no matter
the cost. With their love as their guiding light, they
knew they could overcome any obstacle and achieve a
brighter future for their kingdom.

Chapter 15

The final preparations for the confrontation with Volantis were underway. The defenders of Althea, bolstered by the power of the Philosopher's Stone, were ready to face the enemy with renewed determination. Liora and Kael knew that this battle would be the turning point in the war, and they were prepared to make any sacrifice necessary to protect their homeland.

The morning of the battle dawned cold and clear. The air was charged with tension as the defenders of Althea assembled in the central valley, the site of their previous victory. The valley had been fortified with alchemical defenses, and the protective barrier created by the Philosopher's Stone shimmered faintly in the early light.

Liora stood at the forefront of the army, the Philosopher's Stone in her hand. Its radiant light filled her with a sense of purpose and strength. Kael stood beside her, his presence a reassuring anchor.

"We've faced many challenges to get here," Liora said, her voice steady and clear. "Today, we fight for the future of Althea. We fight for our loved ones, for our homes, and for the peace we seek."

The soldiers and alchemists around her nodded, their faces filled with determination. Commander Aric stepped forward, his voice carrying over the assembled troops. "Today, we stand united. Today, we show Volantis that Althea will not fall. Together, we will achieve victory."

As the enemy forces of Volantis approached, the ground shook with the march of their army. The defenders of Althea braced themselves, their hearts filled with a mixture of fear and resolve. The first clash was imminent, and the valley soon erupted in a cacophony of battle cries, clashing weapons, and the crackle of alchemical energy.

Liora and Kael fought side by side, their movements synchronized and precise. Liora wielded the power of the Philosopher's Stone, creating barriers of fire and ice to protect her comrades and repelling the enemy's advances. Kael, with his martial alchemy, cut through the ranks of Volantis with deadly efficiency.

Despite their efforts, the enemy was relentless. Volantis had brought their most powerful alchemists and warriors, and their attacks were fierce and coordinated. The defenders of Althea fought valiantly, but the sheer number of enemies threatened to overwhelm them.

In the midst of the chaos, Liora spotted a group of enemy alchemists attempting to breach the protective barrier. She knew that if they succeeded, it could spell disaster for Althea's defenses. Determined to stop them, she called out to Kael.

"Kael, we need to stop those alchemists!" she shouted over the din of battle. "If they break the barrier, we're finished."

Kael nodded, his expression resolute. "Let's go, Liora. We'll stop them together."

They fought their way through the chaos, their determination unwavering. As they reached the enemy alchemists, Liora channeled the full power of the Philosopher's Stone, unleashing a wave of energy that disrupted their spells and sent them reeling.

With Kael by her side, Liora faced the enemy alchemists head-on. The battle was fierce, but their combined skills and the power of the Philosopher's Stone gave them the upper hand. One by one, the enemy alchemists fell, and the protective barrier remained intact.

As the battle raged on, Liora and Kael continued to lead the defenders, their presence a beacon of hope and strength. They coordinated the efforts of their allies, using their knowledge of alchemy to create strategic advantages and turn the tide of the battle.

Despite their efforts, the cost was high. Many brave soldiers and alchemists fell in the defense of Althea, their sacrifices a stark reminder of the price of freedom. Liora's heart ached with each loss, but she knew that their sacrifices were not in vain.

As the sun began to set, casting a golden glow over the battlefield, the enemy forces of Volantis began to falter. The defenders of Althea, inspired by the leadership of Liora and Kael, pressed their advantage, driving the enemy back.

In a final, desperate push, the leader of the Volantis forces, a powerful alchemist known as Sorin, stepped forward. His eyes glowed with malevolent energy as he faced Liora and Kael, his voice filled with contempt.

"You think you can defeat me with your pathetic defenses and your little stone?" Sorin sneered. "I will crush you and take the Philosopher's Stone for myself."

Liora's grip tightened around the stone, her eyes filled with determination. "We will protect Althea, no matter the cost. Your reign of terror ends here, Sorin."

The final confrontation was intense and brutal. Sorin unleashed a barrage of dark alchemical spells, each one more powerful and destructive than the last. Liora and Kael fought with everything they had, their movements a blur of skill and power.

Liora channeled the full energy of the Philosopher's Stone, creating barriers and countering Sorin's attacks. Kael fought with unmatched precision, his martial alchemy a deadly force against Sorin's minions. The battlefield shook with the force of their clash, the air filled with the crackle of alchemical energy.

Despite their combined strength, Sorin's power was overwhelming. He managed to break through their defenses, his dark energy striking Liora with a force that sent her sprawling to the ground. The Philosopher's Stone slipped from her grasp, its light dimming as it rolled away.

Kael's eyes widened with fear and anger. "Liora!" he shouted, rushing to her side. He stood protectively over her, his eyes blazing with determination. "You will not touch her, Sorin. I will protect her with my life."

Sorin laughed, his voice filled with malice. "How touching. But your love is no match for my power. Prepare to die."

As Sorin raised his hand to deliver the final blow, Liora struggled to her feet, her heart pounding with determination. She reached out, summoning the power of the Philosopher's Stone. Its light flared brightly, filling her with renewed strength.

With a final, desperate surge of energy, Liora and Kael combined their powers, creating a massive wave of alchemical energy that engulfed Sorin. The force of their combined attack overwhelmed him, and with a final scream, Sorin was consumed by the light, his dark energy dissipating into the air.

The battlefield fell silent as the last echoes of the battle faded away. The defenders of Althea stood in stunned silence, their eyes fixed on Liora and Kael. The protective barrier shimmered brightly, its energy restored by the power of the Philosopher's Stone.

Liora and Kael stood together, their hearts filled with relief and triumph. The battle was over, and they had emerged victorious. The cost had been high, but their sacrifices had not been in vain.

Commander Aric approached them, his face lined with exhaustion and gratitude. "You've done it," he said, his voice filled with emotion. "Your bravery and determination have saved Althea. We owe you everything."

Liora shook her head, her gaze steady. "We did it together, Commander. Every defender here played a part. We will honor their sacrifices and rebuild our homeland."

Kael nodded, his eyes filled with pride and love. "This is just the beginning. We will ensure a future of peace and prosperity for Althea."

As night fell, the defenders of Althea began the somber task of tending to the wounded and honoring the fallen.

The victory was bittersweet, a reminder of the sacrifices made in the name of freedom and peace.

Liora and Kael took a moment to reflect on their journey. They had faced incredible challenges and made great sacrifices, but their determination and unity had carried them through. Their love had been their guiding light, giving them the strength to overcome any obstacle.

With the memory of those they had lost driving them forward, Liora and Kael vowed to continue their fight. They would protect Althea, honor their legacy, and ensure a future of peace and prosperity. The path of the alchemist was one of transformation and enlightenment, but it was also a path of courage, sacrifice, and unity.

The future of Althea depended on it, and Liora and Kael were determined to see it through, no matter the cost. With their love as their guiding light, they knew they could overcome any obstacle and achieve a brighter future for their kingdom.

Chapter 16

The dawn of a new day cast a golden glow over Elaria, marking the end of the long and brutal war. The defenders of Althea had emerged victorious, their unity and determination overcoming the dark forces of Volantis. The battle-scarred land now lay peaceful and still, a testament to the sacrifices made and the courage displayed.

Liora and Kael stood on the balcony of the manor, looking out over the city. The air was filled with a sense of renewal and hope. The people of Althea were beginning to rebuild, their spirits lifted by the promise of a brighter future.

"It's over," Liora said softly, her eyes reflecting a mix of relief and sorrow. "We've won, but the cost was high. So many lives lost, so many sacrifices made."

Kael nodded, his expression somber. "We must honor those who gave their lives for this victory. Their sacrifices were not in vain. Althea will rise stronger and more united than ever before."

The days that followed were filled with the hard work of rebuilding. Liora and Kael, along with the other leaders of Althea, coordinated efforts to restore the city and support the families of those who had fallen. The Philosopher's Stone, its power now fully realized, was used to aid in the reconstruction, its energy healing the land and its people.

Liora spent much of her time in the hidden laboratory, continuing her father's work and exploring the full potential of the Philosopher's Stone. She shared her knowledge with the other alchemists, ensuring that the wisdom and power of alchemy would be used for the good of all.

One evening, as she was working on a particularly complex formula, Kael entered the laboratory. His presence was a comforting anchor, and Liora looked up with a smile.

"How are you feeling?" Kael asked, his voice filled with concern and affection.

Liora sighed, setting aside her work. "I'm tired, but I'm also hopeful. We've accomplished so much, but there's still so much to do. The Philosopher's Stone holds incredible potential, and I want to make sure we use it wisely."

Kael nodded, his eyes reflecting his admiration and love. "You've done incredible work, Liora. Your father would be proud. And I'm proud of you too. We've come so far, and we'll continue to build a better future together."

Liora stood and walked over to Kael, taking his hand in hers. "I couldn't have done any of this without you, Kael. Your support and love have been my strength. Together, we can achieve anything."

Kael smiled, pulling her into a gentle embrace. "I love you, Liora. And I'm excited to see what the future holds for us and for Althea."

As they stood together, the weight of the past months began to lift, replaced by a sense of peace and hope. They knew that the road ahead would still have its challenges, but they were ready to face them together.

In the months that followed, Althea continued to rebuild and prosper. The protective barrier around Elaria, strengthened by the Philosopher's Stone, ensured that the kingdom remained safe from any further threats. The people of Althea, inspired by the bravery and sacrifice of their defenders, worked together to create a future of peace and prosperity.

Liora and Kael's love continued to grow, their bond deepening with each passing day. They spent their days working side by side, using their skills and knowledge to benefit the kingdom. Their evenings were filled with moments of quiet reflection and shared dreams of the future.

One day, as they walked through the gardens of the manor, Liora felt a sense of contentment and fulfillment. The flowers were in full bloom, their vibrant colors a symbol of the renewal and hope that filled the land.

Kael stopped and turned to her, his eyes filled with love. "Liora, we've accomplished so much together. But there's something I've been wanting to ask you."

Liora looked at him, her heart racing. "What is it, Kael?"

Kael took a deep breath, reaching into his pocket and pulling out a small, intricately crafted ring. "Liora, you are my strength, my inspiration, and my love. Will you marry me? Will you be my partner for life, as we continue to build a better future for Althea together?"

Tears filled Liora's eyes as she looked at the ring and then back at Kael. "Yes, Kael. I will marry you. I can't imagine my life without you by my side."

Kael slipped the ring onto her finger, and they embraced, their hearts filled with joy and love. The promise of a shared future, built on the foundation of their love and determination, filled them with hope and excitement.

The news of their engagement brought joy to the people of Althea, who celebrated the union of their beloved leaders. The wedding was a grand and joyous occasion, attended by friends, family, and allies from across the kingdom. It was a symbol of the unity and strength that had carried them through the darkest times.

As they exchanged their vows, Liora and Kael looked into each other's eyes, their hearts filled with love and gratitude. They knew that their journey was far from over, but they were ready to face whatever challenges lay ahead, together.

The path of the alchemist had brought them transformation and enlightenment, but it had also brought them love and unity. With the Philosopher's Stone as their guide, and their love as their strength, they were ready to build a future of peace and prosperity for Althea.

As they stood together, hand in hand, watching the sun set over Elaria, they felt a deep sense of fulfillment and hope. The future of Althea was bright, and they were determined to see it through, no matter the cost.

With their love as their guiding light, Liora and Kael knew they could overcome any obstacle and achieve a brighter future for their kingdom. The journey had been long and challenging, but it had also been filled with moments of joy, love, and triumph.

And as they faced the new dawn together, they knew that the best was yet to come.

Chapter 17

Years passed, and Althea flourished under the leadership of Liora and Kael. The kingdom had been rebuilt stronger and more united than ever, with the teachings of alchemy playing a central role in its prosperity. The Philosopher's Stone, once a symbol of myth and mystery, became a cornerstone of Althea's progress and security.

Liora and Kael had established an alchemical academy where students from all over Althea could come to learn the ancient and powerful craft. The academy was a beacon of knowledge and innovation, dedicated to the principles of balance, transformation, and enlightenment. It was Liora's way of honoring her father's legacy and ensuring that the knowledge he had worked so hard to uncover would be passed on to future generations.

One morning, as Liora stood at the window of her study in the academy, watching the students practice their alchemical skills in the courtyard below, Kael entered the room, carrying a tray with tea and breakfast.

"You've been up early again," Kael said, setting the tray on her desk. "You should take a break and eat something."

Liora turned to him with a smile. "I couldn't sleep. There's so much to do, and I want to make sure everything is perfect for the graduation ceremony next week. These students are our future, and I want them to feel proud of their accomplishments."

Kael walked over and wrapped his arms around her. "They have an incredible mentor and role model in you, Liora. You've done so much for Althea and for these students. Your father's legacy is alive and well because of you."

Liora leaned into his embrace, feeling a sense of peace and fulfillment. "And none of it would have been possible without you, Kael. You've been my rock, my partner, and my greatest support. I'm grateful for every moment we've shared."

As they enjoyed their breakfast together, they discussed the plans for the upcoming ceremony and the future of the academy. Their love and partnership had only grown stronger over the years, and their shared vision for Althea had brought them countless moments of joy and fulfillment.

After breakfast, Liora and Kael made their way to the central hall of the academy, where a group of students was gathered for their final practical exams. The students greeted them with enthusiasm and respect, eager to demonstrate their skills and knowledge.

Liora watched with pride as the students performed complex transmutations, crafted powerful elixirs, and demonstrated their understanding of elemental balance. Each success was a testament to the hard work and dedication they had shown, and Liora knew that the future of alchemy in Althea was in capable hands.

As the exams concluded and the students began to disperse, Liora called out to one of her most promising pupils, a young woman named Elara. Elara had shown exceptional talent and a deep understanding of alchemical principles, reminding Liora of herself when she had first discovered her father's hidden legacy.

"Elara, may I speak with you for a moment?" Liora asked, her voice warm and encouraging.

Elara approached, her eyes filled with admiration and respect. "Of course, Master Liora. What is it you wish to discuss?"

Liora smiled, placing a hand on Elara's shoulder. "I wanted to tell you how proud I am of your progress. You have shown great skill and dedication, and I believe you have the potential to achieve great things. I see in you the same passion and determination that drove me to continue my father's work."

Elara's eyes widened with gratitude. "Thank you, Master Liora. Your guidance and mentorship have meant the world to me. I hope to one day make a difference, just as you have."

"You already are," Liora replied. "And I have a special task for you. There are still many mysteries of alchemy to uncover, and I would like you to lead a new research initiative here at the academy. Your insights and creativity will be invaluable in advancing our understanding and pushing the boundaries of what we know."

Elara's face lit up with excitement. "I would be honored, Master Liora. I won't let you down."

As Elara walked away, filled with a renewed sense of purpose, Liora felt a deep sense of satisfaction. She had fulfilled her father's legacy and had ensured that the knowledge and power of alchemy would continue to grow and thrive in Althea.

Later that evening, Liora and Kael walked through the gardens of their home, enjoying the tranquility and beauty of the night. The stars shone brightly above them, a reminder of the endless possibilities that lay ahead.

"Liora," Kael said, breaking the comfortable silence. "I've been thinking about our journey, everything we've accomplished, and the legacy we've built together. I feel like there's still so much more we can do, not just for Althea, but for the world."

Liora nodded, her eyes reflecting the starlight. "I agree, Kael. Alchemy has the power to transform and enlighten, and we've only just begun to tap into its potential. I believe we can use our knowledge and skills to help other kingdoms, to bring peace and prosperity beyond our borders."

Kael smiled, taking her hand in his. "Then let's do it, together. We'll continue our journey, exploring new horizons and sharing the wisdom of alchemy with those who seek it. Our legacy will be one of love, unity, and the pursuit of knowledge."

As they stood together, hand in hand, looking out at the vast expanse of the night sky, Liora felt a profound sense of fulfillment and hope. The path of the alchemist had brought them transformation and enlightenment, but it had also brought them love and unity.

With their love as their guiding light and the Philosopher's Stone as their compass, Liora and Kael knew they could overcome any obstacle and achieve a brighter future for their kingdom and beyond. The journey had been long and challenging, but it had also been filled with moments of joy, love, and triumph.

As they faced the new dawn together, they knew that the best was yet to come. The legacy of the alchemist would continue to shine brightly, guiding future generations and inspiring them to reach for the stars. Liora and Kael's love and partnership would be remembered as a beacon of hope and strength, a testament to the power of unity and the endless possibilities of alchemy.

And as they walked forward into the future, they knew that their journey was far from over. With each step, they would continue to build a legacy of love, wisdom, and transformation, creating a world where the light of alchemy would shine brightly for all to see.

Chapter 18

Years of peace and prosperity had blessed Althea under the guidance of Liora and Kael. The kingdom had transformed into a beacon of hope and knowledge, thanks to the principles of alchemy and the unity of its people. The Alchemical Academy thrived, producing generations of skilled alchemists who carried forward the legacy of transformation and enlightenment.

One morning, Liora awoke to a sense of anticipation. Today was a significant day—the dedication of the new Alchemical Tower, a structure that symbolized the height of alchemical achievement and the unity of Althea's people. It had taken years to build, a collaborative effort of architects, alchemists, and craftsmen from all over the kingdom.

As Liora dressed, Kael entered the room, his face beaming with excitement. "Today's the day," he said, taking her hands in his. "The Alchemical Tower is finally complete. This is a testament to everything we've worked for."

Liora smiled, feeling a swell of pride and joy. "It's incredible, Kael. I never imagined we would come this far. This tower is more than just a building—it's a symbol of our journey and the legacy we're leaving behind."

The streets of Elaria were filled with festive decorations, and people from all corners of Althea had gathered to witness the dedication ceremony. The atmosphere was electric with excitement and anticipation. Liora and Kael made their way to the tower, greeted by waves of cheers and applause from the crowd.

The Alchemical Tower stood tall and majestic, its spire reaching towards the sky. It was a marvel of engineering and alchemical ingenuity, adorned with intricate carvings and alchemical symbols. At its peak, a crystal orb infused with the essence of the Philosopher's Stone radiated a soft, golden light, visible from miles around.

As they approached the podium, Liora took a moment to reflect on the journey that had brought them here. She thought of her father, whose legacy had been the foundation of their achievements. She thought of the battles they had fought, the sacrifices they had made, and the love that had carried them through it all.

Kael stepped forward, addressing the crowd with a voice filled with pride and emotion. "People of Althea, today we celebrate not just the completion of the Alchemical Tower, but the strength, unity, and determination of our kingdom. This tower stands as a beacon of hope and knowledge, a symbol of what we can achieve when we work together."

Liora joined him, her voice steady and clear. "This tower is a testament to the power of alchemy and the spirit of our people. It represents our commitment to the principles of transformation, enlightenment, and unity. Together, we have built a future where knowledge and love guide us towards a brighter tomorrow."

As they spoke, the crowd erupted in applause, their faces filled with pride and hope. The dedication ceremony continued with performances, speeches, and the unveiling of the tower's interior, which housed a vast library, research laboratories, and spaces for teaching and collaboration.

The day was filled with joy and celebration, a culmination of years of hard work and dedication. As the sun began to set, casting a golden glow over the tower, Liora and Kael stood on the balcony, looking out over the city they had helped rebuild.

"Liora," Kael said, his voice soft and filled with emotion, "we've achieved so much together. This tower, this kingdom—it's all a testament to your vision and determination. I'm so proud of you."

Liora turned to him, her eyes filled with love. "And I'm proud of us, Kael. We've done this together, every step of the way. Our love and partnership have been the foundation of everything we've accomplished."

As they stood together, hand in hand, they felt a profound sense of fulfillment and hope. The future of Althea was bright, and they were ready to continue their journey, exploring new horizons and sharing the wisdom of alchemy with the world.

The following days were filled with visitors from neighboring kingdoms, all eager to learn from Althea's achievements and share their own knowledge. Liora and Kael welcomed them with open arms, fostering a spirit of collaboration and mutual respect.

One evening, as they were walking through the gardens of the academy, Liora felt a sense of peace and contentment. The gardens were filled with the scent of blooming flowers, and the soft glow of lanterns illuminated the paths.

"Liora," Kael said, breaking the comfortable silence, "I've been thinking about our journey, everything we've accomplished, and the legacy we're building. I feel like there's still so much more we can do, not just for Althea, but for the world."

Liora nodded, her eyes reflecting the starlight. "I agree, Kael. Alchemy has the power to transform and enlighten, and we've only just begun to tap into its potential. I believe we can use our knowledge and skills to help other kingdoms, to bring peace and prosperity beyond our borders."

Kael smiled, taking her hand in his. "Then let's do it, together. We'll continue our journey, exploring new horizons and sharing the wisdom of alchemy with those who seek it. Our legacy will be one of love, unity, and the pursuit of knowledge."

As they walked forward, hand in hand, they felt a deep sense of fulfillment and hope. The path of the alchemist had brought them transformation and enlightenment, but it had also brought them love and unity.

With their love as their guiding light and the Philosopher's Stone as their compass, Liora and Kael knew they could overcome any obstacle and achieve a brighter future for their kingdom and beyond. The journey had been long and challenging, but it had also been filled with moments of joy, love, and triumph.

And as they faced the new dawn together, they knew that the best was yet to come. The legacy of the alchemist would continue to shine brightly, guiding future generations and inspiring them to reach for the stars. Liora and Kael's love and partnership would be remembered as a beacon of hope and strength, a testament to the power of unity and the endless possibilities of alchemy.

As they looked out over the horizon, they felt a sense of anticipation and excitement for the future. With their hearts full of love and their spirits unwavering, they were ready to embark on the next chapter of their journey, knowing that together, they could achieve anything.

Chapter 19

In the years following the dedication of the Alchemical Tower, Althea continued to prosper. The kingdom had become a center of knowledge and innovation, attracting scholars, alchemists, and adventurers from far and wide. Liora and Kael, now respected leaders and mentors, oversaw the continued growth of the Alchemical Academy and the implementation of their progressive ideas.

However, peace and prosperity often attract envy and opposition. Rumors began to spread of a rising power in the east, a dark force gathering strength and seeking to challenge Althea's newfound dominance. Whispers of this shadowy threat reached Elaria, and Liora and Kael knew they had to act swiftly to protect their kingdom and the legacy they had built.

One evening, as they sat in the grand library of the Alchemical Tower, poring over ancient texts and maps, a messenger arrived with urgent news. He was a young scout, breathless and covered in dust from his long journey.

"Master Liora, Master Kael," he said, bowing deeply. "I bring dire news from the eastern borders. A powerful army, led by a dark sorcerer named Malachar, is advancing toward Althea. They have already laid waste to several villages and are moving with alarming speed."

Liora and Kael exchanged worried glances. They had heard tales of Malachar, a sorcerer known for his ruthless ambition and mastery of dark magic. His desire for power was insatiable, and his methods were cruel and relentless.

"We need to gather our allies and prepare for battle," Kael said, his voice firm and resolute. "We cannot let Malachar's forces reach Elaria. We must protect our people and our kingdom."

Liora nodded, her mind racing with plans and strategies. "I'll send word to the neighboring kingdoms and request their aid. We must also strengthen our defenses and prepare the alchemists for what lies ahead. This battle will be unlike any we've faced before."

The next few days were a flurry of activity as messengers were dispatched, troops were mobilized, and defenses were fortified. Liora and Kael worked tirelessly, coordinating efforts and rallying their people. The air was thick with tension and anticipation, but also with a sense of unity and determination.

On the eve of the impending battle, Liora stood on the balcony of the Alchemical Tower, looking out over the city she loved so dearly. The stars shone brightly above, a stark contrast to the darkness that loomed on the horizon.

Kael joined her, wrapping an arm around her shoulders. "We've faced many challenges together, Liora. This will be our greatest test yet, but I believe in us. We have the strength and the knowledge to overcome this threat."

Liora leaned into him, drawing comfort from his presence. "We've built something beautiful here, Kael. I won't let Malachar destroy it. We'll fight with everything we have."

The next morning, the people of Althea awoke to the sound of horns signaling the approach of the enemy. Malachar's forces had reached the outskirts of the kingdom, and the time for battle had come.

Liora and Kael led their troops to the front lines, their hearts filled with a mix of fear and resolve. The sight that greeted them was daunting: an army of dark-clad warriors, their eyes burning with malice, led by Malachar himself, a figure shrouded in a cloak of shadow and power.

"People of Althea," Malachar's voice boomed across the battlefield, laced with dark magic. "Surrender now, and your lives will be spared. Resist, and you will face annihilation."

Liora stepped forward, her voice ringing out with unwavering defiance. "We will never surrender to you, Malachar. This is our home, and we will protect it with our lives. Your darkness will not prevail here."

With a roar, the battle began. The clash of swords and the crackle of alchemical energy filled the air as the forces of Althea and Malachar's dark army collided. Liora and Kael fought at the forefront, their skills and determination inspiring those around them.

Liora wielded the power of the Philosopher's Stone, creating barriers of light and energy to protect her allies and repel the enemy's attacks. Kael fought with unmatched precision and strength, his martial alchemy cutting through the ranks of Malachar's warriors.

Despite their efforts, the battle was fierce and relentless. Malachar's dark magic was formidable, and his forces fought with ruthless efficiency. The defenders of Althea were pushed to their limits, their resolve tested with each passing moment.

As the battle raged on, Liora spotted Malachar on a hill overlooking the battlefield, his hands raised in a gesture of dark power. She knew that if they were to have any hope of victory, they needed to confront him directly and break his hold over his army.

"Kael," she called out, her voice urgent. "We need to stop Malachar. He's the source of their strength. If we can defeat him, we can turn the tide of this battle."

Kael nodded, his eyes filled with determination. "I'm with you, Liora. Let's end this."

Together, they fought their way through the chaos, their movements synchronized and purposeful. As they approached the hill, Malachar turned to face them, his eyes glowing with dark energy.

"So, you've come to challenge me," Malachar sneered, his voice dripping with contempt. "You're fools if you think you can defeat me."

"We're not afraid of you," Liora replied, her voice steady and defiant. "Your darkness has no place here. We will protect Althea, no matter the cost."

With a furious cry, Malachar unleashed a torrent of dark magic, but Liora and Kael stood firm. They combined their powers, the light of the Philosopher's Stone clashing with Malachar's darkness in a brilliant display of energy.

The battle between light and dark was intense and unforgiving. Liora and Kael fought with everything they had, drawing on their love and determination to fuel their strength. Malachar's power was overwhelming, but their resolve was unbreakable.

As the clash reached its peak, Liora felt a surge of energy from the Philosopher's Stone. She channeled its power, focusing all her will and intent on breaking Malachar's hold. With a final, desperate effort, she unleashed a wave of light that engulfed the dark sorcerer, shattering his defenses and banishing his darkness.

Malachar let out a scream of rage and pain as his power crumbled, and he was consumed by the light. His army, no longer under his control, faltered and fled, their will broken by the defeat of their leader.

The battlefield fell silent as the last echoes of the battle faded away. The defenders of Althea stood victorious, their faces filled with relief and triumph. Liora and Kael, exhausted but triumphant, embraced each other, their hearts filled with gratitude and love.

"We did it," Liora whispered, her voice choked with emotion. "We've protected Althea."

Kael held her close, his eyes filled with pride. "We did it together, Liora. Our love and determination saw us through. Althea is safe, and we've secured a future of peace."

As the sun set over the battlefield, casting a golden glow over the land, the people of Althea began the process of healing and rebuilding. The victory over

Malachar was a testament to their unity and strength, a reminder that darkness could never triumph over the light.

Liora and Kael stood at the forefront of these efforts, guiding their people with wisdom and compassion. The Alchemical Academy continued to thrive, its halls filled with the laughter and determination of students eager to learn and carry forward the legacy of their mentors.

As the years passed, the story of Liora and Kael's love and their battle against Malachar became legend, inspiring future generations to strive for greatness and to always stand united against the forces of darkness.

One evening, as they walked through the gardens of their home, Liora felt a deep sense of peace and fulfillment. The stars shone brightly above, a reminder of the endless possibilities that lay ahead.

"Kael," she said, her voice soft and filled with emotion, "we've accomplished so much together. Our journey has been long and challenging, but it's also been filled with moments of joy, love, and triumph."

Kael smiled, taking her hand in his. "And there's still so much more to do, Liora. Together, we'll continue to build a legacy of love, wisdom, and transformation. The future of Althea is bright, and I'm excited to see what lies ahead."

As they stood together, hand in hand, looking out at the vast expanse of the night sky, Liora felt a profound sense of hope and anticipation for the future. The path of the alchemist had brought them transformation and enlightenment, but it had also brought them love and unity.

With their love as their guiding light and the Philosopher's Stone as their compass, Liora and Kael knew they could overcome any obstacle and achieve a brighter future for their kingdom and beyond. The journey had been long and challenging, but it had also been filled with moments of joy, love, and triumph.

And as they faced the new dawn together, they knew that the best was yet to come. The legacy of the alchemist would continue to shine brightly, guiding future generations and inspiring them to reach for the stars. Liora and Kael's love and partnership would be remembered as a beacon of hope and strength, a testament to the power of unity and the endless possibilities of alchemy.

As they walked forward, hand in hand, they felt a deep sense of fulfillment and hope. With their hearts full of love and their spirits unwavering, they were ready to embark on the next chapter of their journey, knowing that together, they could achieve anything.

Epilogue

The victory over Malachar had secured a lasting peace for Althea. The kingdom, now a beacon of alchemical knowledge and enlightenment, continued to flourish under the guidance of Liora and Kael. The Alchemical Academy became a renowned institution, attracting students and scholars from distant lands who sought to learn from the wisdom of Althea.

Liora and Kael's love and partnership had not only saved their kingdom but had also set a standard for leadership rooted in compassion, wisdom, and unity. Their legacy was etched into the very fabric of Althea, a shining example of what could be achieved through determination, love, and the transformative power of alchemy.

Years passed, and Liora and Kael grew older, their hair touched with silver, but their hearts and spirits remained as vibrant as ever. They had dedicated their lives to ensuring the prosperity and enlightenment of Althea, and now, their thoughts turned towards the future and the legacy they would leave behind.

One day, as they walked through the bustling halls of the Alchemical Academy, Liora and Kael were approached by Elara, their most promising pupil who had become a respected alchemist and teacher in her own right.

"Master Liora, Master Kael," Elara said, bowing respectfully. "The students and I have been working on a project to honor your contributions to Althea and to celebrate the legacy you've built. We would like to show you."

Curious and touched, Liora and Kael followed Elara to the central courtyard of the academy. There, the students had gathered around a magnificent sculpture made of crystal and precious metals, shaped like a towering spire with intricate alchemical symbols etched into its surface. At the top of the spire, a radiant crystal orb infused with the essence of the Philosopher's Stone glowed brightly.

"This is the Monument of Unity," Elara explained, her eyes shining with pride. "It symbolizes the unity, knowledge, and love that you have brought to Althea. It will stand here as a reminder to all future generations of the principles you have taught us and the legacy you have created."

Liora's eyes filled with tears as she looked at the beautiful monument. "It's incredible, Elara. Thank you. This means more to us than words can express."

Kael nodded, his heart swelling with pride. "You've all done an amazing job. This monument will inspire future generations to continue our work and uphold the values we've fought for."

The dedication of the Monument of Unity was a joyous occasion, attended by people from all over Althea and beyond. The celebrations lasted for days, filled with music, performances, and heartfelt speeches honoring Liora and Kael's legacy.

As the festivities came to an end, Liora and Kael found a moment of quiet reflection. They stood before the monument, hand in hand, gazing up at the glowing crystal orb.

"We've accomplished so much, Kael," Liora said softly. "Our journey has been filled with challenges and triumphs, but it's also been filled with love and joy. I'm grateful for every moment we've shared."

Kael squeezed her hand, his eyes filled with love. "And I'm grateful for you, Liora. Together, we've built something beautiful and lasting. Our love and partnership have made all of this possible."

Their lives continued to be filled with purpose and fulfillment, guiding the academy and mentoring the next generation of alchemists. They traveled to other kingdoms, sharing their knowledge and fostering alliances that ensured lasting peace and prosperity.

One evening, as they sat together on the balcony of their home, watching the sun set over Elaria, Liora felt a sense of peace and contentment. The sky was painted in hues of gold and pink, a symbol of the beauty and wonder of the world they had helped create.

"Kael," Liora said, her voice filled with emotion, "we've lived a remarkable life. Our journey has been extraordinary, and our love has been the greatest gift of all. As we look to the future, I feel at peace knowing that our legacy will continue through the lives we've touched and the knowledge we've shared."

Kael nodded, his heart filled with gratitude. "We've created a legacy of love, wisdom, and transformation. And while our journey may be coming to an end, the impact we've made will endure. Future generations will carry forward the torch of alchemy, guided by the principles we've instilled."

In the twilight of their lives, Liora and Kael continued to find joy and fulfillment in their work and in each other. They spent their days surrounded by the people they loved, passing on their wisdom and cherishing the moments of quiet reflection.

As the years went by, they witnessed the continued growth and prosperity of Althea. The academy flourished, and the teachings of alchemy spread far and wide, bringing enlightenment and transformation to countless lives.

One peaceful morning, Liora and Kael passed away, holding hands and surrounded by their loved ones. Their passing was a moment of profound sadness, but also a celebration of two lives well-lived and a love that had transcended time.

The people of Althea mourned their loss but honored their memory by continuing their work and upholding the values they had taught. The Monument of Unity stood as a testament to their legacy, a beacon of hope and inspiration for future generations.

In the years that followed, the story of Liora and Kael became legend, their names spoken with reverence and admiration. Their love and partnership were remembered as a shining example of what could be achieved through unity, determination, and the transformative power of alchemy.

And so, the legacy of the alchemist and the warrior lived on, a source of inspiration for all who sought to create a better world. Liora and Kael's journey had been one of transformation and enlightenment, but it had also been one of love and unity. Their story would forever be a beacon of hope, guiding future generations towards a brighter, more enlightened future.

As the sun set over Althea, casting a golden glow over the land, the spirit of Liora and Kael lived on in the hearts and minds of the people they had touched. Their legacy was eternal, a testament to the power of love, unity, and the endless possibilities of alchemy.

And as the stars began to twinkle in the night sky, the people of Althea looked to the future with hope and determination, knowing that the legacy of the alchemist and the warrior would continue to guide them towards a brighter tomorrow.

www.ingramcontent.com/pod-product-compliance
Lightning Source LLC
Chambersburg PA
CBHW071017180726
48291CB00004B/1510